Bloody Seas

Edited by Jeff Byrne
Cover illustration by cakikandy

To the
Donald J. Bingle
For your wonderful help

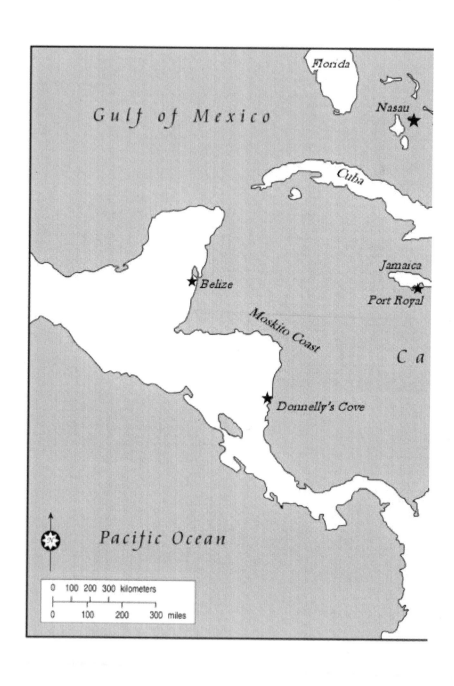

Atlantic Ocean

Bahama Islands

Greater
Antilles

Hispaniola

Puerto Rico

Lesser
Antilles

Montserrat

Caribbean Sea

Martinique

Barbados

Maracaibo

Spanish Main

Moskito Coast

"And what was it made you think I'd take in more lost sheep?" This time Conner Donnelly gave no pretense of greeting honored guests. His best coat was somewhere else, and his shirt sleeves were rolled to the elbow. Scarlet considered it a victory that she had made her way as far as his office. The four slaves who had rowed ashore with her still stood on the beach, with Burgess and Dark Maire bracketing them and Conner's brother Sean holding them all at gunpoint.

Scarlet licked her lips. "It's a hot day, love. Give us a pint of beer?"

"I will not. Your last lot are drinking it as fast as we can make it. And eating us right off the beach."

"No grand thing goes easy. You know that. But your city's going up. What's that lovely structure back on the hill?"

Conner's eyes flashed. "It's a church, if you can't tell from the great cross they've raised up beside it. A bloody church, because you had to bring me a bloody priest..." His voice had been rising, and he cut himself off suddenly and looked around, before continuing in a much softer tone. "As if I didn't have work and danger on every side, food to be caught and ships to be sunk, and natives watching us from the woods. Now I have a Holy Father with no confidence in my means of livelihood or the state of my soul."

Scarlet leaned in and whispered. "And what was I supposed to do with him? Throw him into the ocean? Hand him over to Ned Doyle?"

At mention of Doyle, Conner shut his eyes for a moment, but when he opened them he did not seem more sociable. "The priest wants to reform me."

"A cooper wants to sell barrels. That don't mean you have to buy 'em."

"He's a priest, and his flock is with him. It ain't easy." Conner sighed. "The man's pretty damn close to getting control of this stretch of beach clean away from me. I may have to move."

"Conner, not that!"

"I tell you, the last time we set out a signal fire, the good father walked down the beach and put it out. Mick hauled him off, but then all those folk with him was angry. They're like to drive us all off our own land."

Scarlet shifted uneasily. "Have you spoken to the man?"

"A priest? If it's so easy, why don't you do it?"

"Well, he was on my ship four days. I do know him a bit."

Conner stood and leaned over the desk, hovering over Scarlet, his shoulders looming. "You get the good father calmed down, and I'll think about taking on this next lot. Not before."

Scarlet looked at her knuckles for a while, glanced up at Conner and finally said, "As you will." She had never argued with a priest before.

It was a long, hot tramp back into the brush, the air still and the path clogged with palmetto fronds that tore at Scarlet's clothes and skin. She found her way by keeping an eye up to the rough tower with its looming cross, taller than the great trees that surrounded it.

The work site was cleared of trees and brush, and Scarlet paused for a moment in the last of the forest's shade before going on. She wished she could shed some clothes, but it did not seem a wise choice when going to talk to a priest. Instead, she unpinned her skirt and let it fall to its full length, covering her ankles. Then she stepped out into the glare.

She found Father Patrick standing on a pile of dirt while those around him rested, hiding from the blistering sun under scrub trees and palms. He had contrived a rough black cassock from somewhere, and a silver cross hung on his chest. He had covered his head with a wide straw hat, but his face was burned red. Scarlet dropped a curtsey, and looked into his eyes. Fierce enough, but with no taint of sunstroke or madness.

"Yes, Captain MacGrath?"

"I've come to speak to you, Father, about your situation." Out in the sun, the heat was worse. Sweat ran down Scarlet's neck and between her breasts.

"What?" Father Patrick swatted at a mosquito. "We're raising a church here, to show our gratitude to God and dig ourselves into this new land."

"And may I ask what else are your parishioners doing? Folk cannot eat a church."

"We have built homes. The women plant and gather. This new land is bountiful." He shifted, looking down from his pile of dirt.

Scarlet swallowed. It was most unpleasant to look up at him, with the pale sky like white-hot iron behind. "And do you help to man the cannons by the cove mouth?" she asked. "Do you trade?"

"We have not come to that yet."

"Nor will you. It's a matter for the governor of this land."

At this Father Patrick came down off his dirt, wiped his forehead with a cloth and stared at her, making her sweat even more. "What? That boy? He is a pirate and a murderer. He lights false signal-fires along the coast, and means to wreck passing ships. He'll bring the law or the wrath of God down upon us all."

A tart remark rose to Scarlet's lips, but she held it back. Instead, she dropped her eyes, then looked up slowly. "It seems to me, Father, that we do our share of good. You was all saved for that we took that ship of yours as a prize."

"It was God's hand moving you, lass. And now I need to bring the same upon these barbarians."

Scarlet could remember the results of other false signal fires, the dead bodies washing up on the beach. She sighed. "He does it because he need to, Father. It ain't like he enjoys it."

"And that cleans his soul? What about the women these scamps chase, or... " Father Patrick paused and looked sharply up the trail that Scarlet had come by. A little girl, her hair in braids, her skirt and blouse apparently made from some of Conner's trade silk, came running up. "Father," she curtsied, then paused, looking frightened. "Conner says to bring everyone back to the shore."

"And now the young villain is ordering me about!" The priest pounded a fist into his left palm and glared at Scarlet as if she was somehow responsible for Conner.

Scarlet was looking at the girl, who stood on one bare foot, rubbing her ankle on the back of the opposite calf. "What's all the rush?"

The girl looked nervously between Scarlet and the priest. "I don't know, mum. His brother Mick came in from the forest and then he sent me to bring you."

The priest was beginning to turn turkey red in the face, and Scarlet raised a placating hand. "Father, this don't seem like Conner's regular way of doing business. Give the man a chance and come in. Besides, it's hot as… hot enough to… hot enough to fry an egg on a stone, it is. Come back to the shore and have a drink.

One of the laborers, sitting on a fallen tree, called out, "It's fearsome hot, Father, and we could all stand with a drink."

Scarlet did her best to be persuasive without flirting. "The surf's cool and the sea breeze is blowing. Your men can't do no more work 'til sunset, or they'll drop like flies. Get 'em someplace cool."

"All right, all right." Father Patrick glared at Scarlet, but took off his straw hat and waved it to the lounging worker. They gathered up their gear so quickly that Scarlet suspected they'd been looking for an excuse for some time.

Scarlet was first back to the beach, but the scene was much different from when she had walked away from it an hour ago. Now the huts, the shade-tress and the beach itself were crowded with people. A quick glance told her that they could be none but the former slaves. When she had seen them last they had been pale and thin, their clothes stained from their confinement. Now they were tanned and freckled by the sun, wearing odd combinations of sailcloth, trade silk and Indian cotton. Men, women and children, they crowded Conner's settlement like ants on a hill.

She pushed her way through the crowd and finally found Conner, standing with Mick halfway into the jungle. "What the devil's up?"

"Natives." Conner held a long rifle, and Mick was bleeding from a wound on his head. "They attacked Mick in the woods."

"I didn't give 'em no cause to fire first, but I did fire after." Mick glared at Scarlet as if she had accused him of something. "Bastards just shot me out of nowhere. We fired back, and I think we got one."

"You should have tried talking." Conner looked from Mick to Scarlet, his brow furrowed. "The locals are pretty friendly, mostly. We trade with 'em. They've never offered to fight before, even when there's been arguments about women and such."

"What did you do to them?" Scarlet demanded, looking at Mick.

"Not a thing. We were hunting wild pigs. We do it all the time. They just shot me, and yelled something, and ran off."

"What are natives doing with guns?" Scarlet glared at Mick.

"They've always had, 'em," Conner said. "They had a few when we came here, and we've traded them for more. A musket's worth twenty goats or fifteen pigs."

Scarlet gaped at him. "You've given guns to a lot of savages?"

Conner turned on her. "They ain't savages. They're folks, and they've been right good to us. Speak English, and anxious to trade fair. They ain't been like this before."

"Well they're like this now!" Mick waved his fist in Conner's face. "Will you give me a bigger party to go out and deal with 'em or not?"

Conner opened his mouth to reply, but the sharp "pang!" of a gunshot rang out in the distance and he paused. Scarlet stood beside him, watching and listening, as something came toward them, crashing and ripping through the brush. Conner pulled a pistol from his belt, and Scarlet reached into her coat pockets for her own guns.

It was a group of people. Scarlet could hear their footsteps and their occasional cries. From further back in the brush more gunshots rang out. Mick pulled a knife with a jagged, ugly blade, and Conner turned the hunting rifle in his hands to wield it like a club.

Ten feet away, the first body broke from between the trees. It was an Irishwoman, with hair nearly as bright as Scarlet's own, her hands filthy, her face scratched and torn, her eyes wild. She shouted in Irish, and Conner lowered his weapon.

A half-dozen more women, some still clutching baskets of fruit, began to scramble out of the trees, and ran past them to join family nearer the beach. Then the woods became unnaturally silent. No bird song, no sounds of animals. Scarlet caught herself holding her breath. Another gunshot, not very far away this time. Then a wild voice shrieked something in a language Scarlet did not know. Silence descended again.

The women were babbling that they had been chased by wild men. Several of them were bloodied by their flight through the brush, but none seemed badly hurt.

Conner turned to Scarlet.

"Damn all priests! If we had put up a fort as I wanted, we'd be ready for this. Instead we've got that bloody tower and a half-finished church…"

"What is going on here?" demanded Father Patrick, striding toward them between the huts.

Conner rounded on him. "What have you lot been up to? Have you been plaguing the native folk, and them done nothing to you?"

"I hardly knew there were such people about. What are they doing attacking our women-folk at their labors?"

"As long as you ain't been stirring these folk up, I'll keep you under my protection now." Conner looked sharply around the group, and then out toward the trees. "We've got no defenses on this side. It's all set up to fight off folk coming into the cove. Scarlet, can you bring the *Donnybrook* up and…"

Scarlet gritted her teeth. "I will not. I'm nothing to you but business, Conner. You made that clear when you ask for gold to help a priest and his people out of slavery. You ain't Irish-hearted." A tear was welling up in her eye, but she blinked it back. "I owe you nothing."

Conner clenched his jaw. "So you'll leave us all to die here, if the natives come?"

"I'll deal, same as you did."

Conner stared into her eyes. "Well, what do you want," he asked, "To save women and children from an attack?"

He knew the thought of children would get to her, but she refused to show it. "If the *Donnybrook* comes into this, it must be because the crew votes to do it. Getting out of here's just saving our skins, I don't need a vote on that."

"You can make them vote as you please."

"Sometimes. What do you offer?"

Father Patrick looked from one to the other. "You're arguing? Making deals, when those savages are gathering to attack?"

Scarlet didn't bother to look around. "Welcome to the Caribbean, Father. We're all here to save our own skins, it seems. Conner, what do you offer to me and mine? I've got cannons, and I can bring 'em in close and shoot over the huts into the jungle."

Conner's sand-fort and cannons stretched for eighty feet along the shore, with the collection of huts and Conner's office and warehouse behind it. It offered little defense from attacks from the jungle, but Scarlet was pretty sure she could get enough elevation on the guns to fire over the huts and reach the trees.

Conner scowled. "What do you want?"

"I want you to take this lot off my hands, and treat 'em fair. And I want my hold full of food and water. And if there's another lot, someday, you take them too. Then you'll be acting like an Irishman, and not like some bloody Spanish war-lord."

"If there is a third lot, you won't be dealing with me. I'll be chased off my land by this priest, if not dead by the hand of some fool who thinks I've offended Mother Church."

"Do I have your word?"

"As long as I'm alive."

Scarlet looked into his eyes. "Then get me Burgess and Dark Maire from wherever you've got 'em stowed. I'll row out to the *Donny* and do my best to get your vote."

The *Donnybrook's* crew was already watching the settlement with interest. Men and women, brightly dressed in anticipation of on-shore revelry, stood along the railing, or perched in the rigging, necks craned and hands shielding their eyes from the blazing tropical sun.

As soon as the longboat brushed the ship's side, Scarlet clambered up the boarding ladder. "Quit gawking!" she commanded. "Mister Flynn, kindly set up the capstan. Jimmy Beason, prepare to drop a kedge-anchor. William, get off that cannon, they're for fighting, not for standing on."

"But I can't see…"

"Can you tell us what's about?" The Shantyman looked as concerned as anyone.

Scarlet chose her words carefully. She had told Conner there must be a vote, but she would avoid one if she could. "We need to come about so we can fire into the jungle. Natives suddenly decided to move against Conner. The *Donny* will support him from here, and I'll take volunteers with firearms ashore."

Sunny Jim crossed his arms over his chest and Beason stood staring, his mouth hanging open. A few others shifted restlessly. "What's in it for us?" Sunny Jim asked.

Scarlet looked around her. "Now see here. You was all for rescuing folk when the mood was on you, and cash in your pockets. Well, this is what comes of it. We left people ashore here, and we mean to leave more. Doin' so makes us responsible-like."

The Shantyman cleared his throat. "Meaning no disrespect, Captain, but a native uprising… Someone could get hurt."

Scarlet turned to the gunnery master. "Mister Bracegirdle, you looking for an excuse to fire them cannons?"

"Always, Ma'am."

Scarlet turned to the rest of them. "It ain't my plan to get anyone killed. But Conner's been a good friend to us in the past, and we're about to ask another favor of him. Let's warp the boat around so we can do him some good."

One of the former slaves, Kian, a middle-aged man with a face weathered by the sun, his reddish hair bleached almost white, wearing the remnants of a linen shirt and a coat handed down to him by Flynn, came forward, asking in Irish, "This is this is place where you mean to leave us?"

"It is." Scarlet glanced toward the shore, looking at the long ridge of packed sand and two lonely cannons that served the place as a fort-wall, the uneven string of palmetto-thatched huts ranged behind it, the sea-wrack cobbled together to make the supply-barn, and wondered what the place looked like to someone just come over from the home country.

Kian's weathered face was blank of expression. Scarlet reckoned he was not seeing the pirate's description of a "growing city" in the rough settlement. Her own remembrances of Ireland had faded with time, but she recalled stone buildings and plowed fields. Conner didn't even have stone to build with, and if the last lot of refuges had managed to plant anything, she hadn't seen it.

But wondering about Conner's settlement would have to wait. Just now she had a battle to plan. She looked back into the faces of her crew. "We'll just haul the *Donny* around on a cable, and fire if anything comes in range. We have powder and shot. I ain't asking anyone to get their hands dirty."

Pryce stepped forward. "Well, what are we waiting for? You're always at such pains to tell me of the superiority of the Irish race. D'you not like to fight any more?"

That brought a ragged laugh. Scarlet began to breathe easy again. "Well? Get me that kedge-anchor out, and let's bring her to bear on the shore. Load up the guns."

The pirates went to work. Bracegirdle's gun crews gathered around the cannons. Flynn selected an anchor and Yeboah carried it down to the longboat.

With the second anchor set at a distance, the capstan crew began to work the big, man-powered winch, and the ship turned slowly around until she hung between her fore and aft lines, rocking gently with the waves.

Bracegirdle's crews pulling canvas covers off the big guns, sponging them out and hauling shot and equipment up on deck. William headed below to begin bringing up powder. It was an organized sort of chaos, and one which the *Donnybrook* had seen many times before.

Scarlet ran up on the bowsprit and looked over at Conner's settlement. A crowd of people surged and churned along the line of huts, some screaming in fear, others blank-faced. Conner's people, the bond-slaves and Africans and natives who had lived among the Donnellys for years, scampered about through the crush, wetting huts with seawater and dragging the cannons back toward the jungle. The priest was nowhere to be seen. .

No attack from the jungle.

Her own ship hardly needed her attention. The *Donnybrook* lay secured by her cables, an unmoving, floating gun platform. The crew knew their business. It was the activity on shore drew her. From her place on the bowsprit, she shouted. "*Donnybrooks* all! Who'll go ashore with me?"

The crew stopped what they were doing, stopped sighting cannon and carrying shot and putting away the capstan-staves, and stared at her. No volunteers. Damn. Scarlet began to wonder if ferrying slaves had made them soft, if they needed a sea-battle to turn their blood red again.

But up from below came Kian, with several of his fellows behind him, and two women among the group. Kian stuck out his chin and spoke. "It it's volunteers you're asking for, then let us be the first of them. We're to live in this place, the best way to make it our home is to plant a little Irish blood in the soil. God help us, we may have been dragged from our homeland, but we still know how to fight."

"That's the spirit this boat used to have," Scarlet shouted, looking around the deck. "Anyone else with us?" Her crew stood silent. "All right then, but see what judgment heaven sends you, for ignoring your fellows. Bring the longboat back around. I'm going to shore."

The *Donnybrook* held a supply of muskets and small-arms that were common property, and the former slaves had been taught to use them when they first came aboard. Scarlet handed out the guns, picked up her sword and six pistols, and loaded sixteen of the former captives into the longboat before climbing in herself. As she was reaching for the oars, Mister Yeboah's vast form came down the ladder and stepped gently into the boat. The longboat's stern sank until the wavelets lapped up over the gun'le, and Yeboah knelt, careful as a draft horse on a narrow trail.

The landsmen moved forward, a nervous gesture that nonetheless balanced the boat. As they pulled away, Scarlet grinned and shouted up to Pryce, "Keep my boat safe and don't sail away without me, you damned English."

Pryce stuck her head over the railing and matched the grin. "We'll be here. Just don't die in the bloody jungle, you damned Irish rebel."

Back inland, the air hung hot, still and humid as a boiled blanket. Yeboah's dark form gleamed with sweat. Scarlet lifted her hair up and shoved it under her hat.

The Donnelly boys stood behind the string of huts, clutching weapons and peering into the jungle.

"Anything?" Scarlet asked.

Conner shrugged. "Not much. We have the boat?"

"She's lined up to fire. I'm here. And your new settlers have guns and are awaiting your word to fight."

"Faith." Conner didn't take his eyes from the trees, but the muscle in his jaw clenched. "That's what you do."

"That's what I do. For a friend."

Mick scowled. "Ain't you a couple? Well, don't start slappin' skin anytime soon. We need to take out some of these bastards."

Scarlet glanced at him. "Maybe it was some kind of mistake."

"Bastards shot at me."

"Maybe they mistook you for a pig."

Mick stepped forward with his fist raised, and Scarlet raised her own, but Yeboah's vast hand reached out from behind her and caught Mick by the sleeve. "Don' be strikin' my captain," The African's face was peaceful, impassive, but a crescent of white glittered at the corner of his eye. Mick tried to shake himself loose, muttered something, and stepped back. Yeboah let him go.

Conner signaled for Mick to come to his side, but Mick ignored him. Conner sighed mightily. "The natives have been different for a while now. I didn't want to believe it was true, not with all the other troubles, but they don't like that we have so many people here. They've been odd, not coming to trade, acting like they're afraid. We hear 'em speaking together, in the jungle, but we don't see 'em."

Behind them, between the huts, a small disturbance swirled, and Father Patrick's voice boomed. "What are you young blackguards up to now? Stirring up the natives to violence?"

The muscles along Conner's jaw tightened. "With all due respect, Father, sit down and shut your gob."

The priest's black robe appeared from between two huts and he continued his approach, voice raised. "I would if I had any trust in you, you rascal. Have you been trifling with the native girls, in addition to your other sins?

"This settlement goes on as it always has," Conner's face was hard, though he never took his eyes from the trees. "The only thing different is you." He went silent. Something crashed in the brush.

Father Patrick looked nervously about, lowered his head and began to pray. Scarlet crossed herself for luck and kept her eyes open. The crashing came nearer and nearer. She heard shots and porcine squeals.

Something was coming in fast, and low to the ground. A boar burst through a screen of palmetto fronds, ears twisted in rage, white tusks gleaming, and head down. Scarlet shot and heard it squeal, then leveled her next pistol. The animal turned in its flight and crashed into the man beside her, knocking him to the ground tearing into his belly.

Scarlet shot it again, this time in the head, but the thing refused to die, digging into its victim with tusks and forefeet while the man writhed and shrieked. Muskets and pistols were firing all along the line, as more animals raced out of the underbrush.

The boar finally left its bloody victim and turned on Scarlet. She backed up fast, struggled to get the next pistol from her pocket. The boar was covered in blood, its little red pig-eyes burning with rage, the tail corkscrewing wildly. Scarlet got her pistol clear, fired and missed, and then the thing was on her, ripping her skirts to shreds, tearing at her coat. This close, the tusks looked like sabers.

She didn't have room to draw her sword. Instead she pulled the marlin spike from her belt and began punching it into the beast's face, aiming for the eyes. The heavy feet pounded against her thighs and belly.

Then the pig was off her. Yeboah lifted it by the hind legs, took half a dozen steps and swung it into the side of a hut. The grass wall collapsed, but one corner post stood, and Yeboah swung the pig over and over, pounding its head and body into the post until it finally went limp.

Father Patrick knelt by the side of the fallen man, murmuring and closing his eyes. All along the battle line, men lay screaming or moaning. Dead and dying pigs littered the ground. Then Scarlet smelled smoke. A native stood atop the hut behind them, a lighted torch in his hand, trying to fire the palmetto thatch of the roof. The green fronds smoldered and began to catch.

A shot rang out from the far side, and the native warrior fell. Then Scarlet's ear caught the deep "poom" of cannon fire. It was the *Donny's* guns. The hut roof collapsed in a spray of thatch and splinters. Another hut fell.

Conner was screaming curses. Scarlet added her own voice. "Get down!" Four more shots buried themselves in the Donnelly's homes.

Mick ran screaming toward the shore, waving a cutlass as if to rush out into the water and attack the ship. Scarlet followed him, her legs tangling in the torn remnants of her skirt. The other side of the row of huts she could see dozens of people cowering behind the sand barricade, hands over their ears or faces, praying or screaming or rocking back and forth.

Scarlet leaped to the top of the barricade and made a speaking-tube of her hands. "Cease firing!" she bellowed, so loud she could feel the strain on her throat.

Conner emerged from between two huts, pistol in one hand, sword in the other. When he saw Scarlet he shouted, "What the hell are they doing?"

"They couldn't see." The gun crews were standing still as oxen. Scarlet turned back toward Conner. "The deal was, they'd fire when they saw we was in trouble. Usually that means powder-smoke, but we was behind the huts and mostly fighting with swords and knives. When they seen that fellow tryin' to fire the roofs, they thought it was time to let fly."

"Well, they've done more damage than the natives." Conner looked around. "Everybody, reload! Get the wounded to cover! How many still standing?"

Perhaps two dozen answered. Men and a few women were staggering back from the battle line limping or clutching wounds to arms or bodies. Conner waded into the surf and pulled at Mick's shoulder. "Get back here. I need you here." Mick continued to glare at the ship, but came away with his brother.

Too many of the folk from the colony seemed to have no fight in them. Men, women and children lay along the shore, even as others kept watch, or reloaded firearms. Father Patrick came carrying a wounded man toward the beach, and a few women got up to help him.

Scarlet gave one more wave to the *Donny* and moved back toward the jungle. The fighters were Conner's original settlers, folk who had come to him with nothing to recommend them but a pair of light heels and a talent for not getting caught. They had looted wrecks along the shore for years, and seen that there were no survivors. They were as scrappy as folk came.

The man who had stood at Scarlet's left lay in the dirt, eyes closed, white and still. Scarlet recognized one of her latest load of escaped slaves, though she couldn't remember the man's name. Kian had said that Irish blood would hold the land. She hoped it would be so. This one was dead, even though he was still breathing. The smell of his ruptured intestines left no doubt.

The defenders began to form up again. Father Patrick had formed a group to pull the badly wounded under cover. Scarlet listened to the priest's words, wishing she could remember the fallen man's name. Well, someone would remember.

Conner called out to the hoard shivering by the sand wall, calling for them to bring sea water and wet down the huts again. A few rose and began to make halfhearted efforts. Scarlet felt thirst sticking her tongue to the roof of her mouth. "Conner," she called, "Find us a bucket of water."

He stood in a gap between the huts, looking back and forth, sword ready and pistol stuck into his belt. "Wait. I need to find Sean."

Scarlet began to scan the faces of the defenders. She saw Kian, some of his fellows, the woman who had fought with them. No Sean.

No Yeboah.

His dark head should have stood well above anyone in the camp, but she could not see him. She called, "Mister Yeboah!" but heard no answer. She strode back and forth, looking between huts, staring into the darkness between, calling his name.

Conner was calling too, Sean's name, over and over.

"Those bastards took him." Mick still held a guard position, staring into the jungle. "They took him. They're dragging people off now."

Conner went to him, and looked into the jungle. "Did you see anything?"

"I don't hafta, now do I? Them natives, them damn bastards, they took him. They musta come in while we were fighting them pigs, they took Sean and he's gone. We should get muskets and the rest of the gunpowder and go in there and kill every one of 'em. Burn the whole feckin' jungle."

Conner's face was drawn with worry. "Just calm down."

"Calm down? While they're out in the jungle, torturing my brother? Don't you give a care for family anymore?"

Conner made a fist as if to strike his brother, but pounded it into his own hand instead. "Maybe he wandered off someplace...."

Mick's face twisted with rage and scorn. "Sean ain't bright but..."

Scarlet broke in. "My man Yeboah's gone, too, and he ain't small enough to be taken easy. Any chance they tried to circle around somehow?"

Mick turned on her with an expression of contempt, but it was Conner that spoke. "Circle where? It's jungle from here to the Floridas."

Scarlet made a helpless gesture. "Yeboah's too big to be took, I tell you, and he's too bright to run off. Any chance Sean ran from the pigs, and Yeboah went after him?"

Mick roared and went for her, and Scarlet fended him off with her sword. When Conner didn't step in to break them up, Scarlet shouted for Mick to back off, and finally drew a pistol. "Mick, stop it for God's sake. If we're to get your brother back, we must work together."

A woman beside one of the huts started keening. The sharp, painful sound of anguish brought Mick to a stop. He turned to his brother. "Give me the guns and fix us up some torches. I'll kill everything in that jungle..."

Conner shook his head. "There's too many dead and hurt already, and we've got no proof…"

"Hey!" A cheerful voice shouted from fifty yards down the beach. "Hey, I got one!"

Scarlet spun and stared. It looked like Sean, and the man with him was definitely Yeboah, dragging a third figure who seemed to be a child. Mick ran toward them, and when he reached Sean, knocked him into the sand and began to pummel him with his fists.

Conner looked the area over one more time, stared into the trees for a moment, then headed toward his brothers, pulled Mick off, and slapped Sean on the head with his open hand. Scarlet glanced back to the jungle, saw that Kian still stood guard, with a group of men around him, and sauntered down the beach to join the brothers.

She nodded a greeting to Yeboah. The person in his hands was brown and small, and as nearly naked as Scarlet had seen a human out among folks. The boy worn only the smallest possible bit of fabric, a necklace of strung teeth, and a headdress of feathers in his short, carefully styled hair.

When the child caught her looking at him he stood straighter, raised a fist and said something she couldn't understand. Yeboah tightened his grip on the boy's arm until it looked painful. The boy's eyes flashed discomfort for a mere second, and then he stood, head high, glaring at them all.

Once Conner and Mick had finished pounding on their brother, they all stood together and took stock. Sean beamed with pleasure. "I seen these fellers out in the brush, and went down to have a look. This one come out to fight, and me and Yeboah caught him between us and brung him in."

Scarlet looked to Yeboah's eyes for confirmation, and received the smallest of shrugs. It had happened about like that. She turned back to the Donnellys.

Mick stood with his hands braced on his hips, beaming. "Well, my little brother finally does somethin' right."

"That he does!" said Conner. "Now we can find out what's at the bottom of this."

Mick rubbed the side of his face. "You think to keep the kid a hostage, or torture him?"

"I think no such thing." Conner caught the boy by the upper arm, so firmly that Yeboah let go his own grip, and led the child back towards the huts. The boy moved with tremendous, injured dignity. Conner asked him a question, and was answered by a string of words in the native tongue.

Conner looked back to Scarlet and Yeboah, who were following at a convenient distance. "I'm pretty sure he's the chief's son. His da speaks English. If we threaten this one just a little, we may be able to get something out of his da."

Scarlet nodded. The shadows were growing longer, but it was no cooler than it had been at noon. In fact, with the breeze beginning to die, it was worse. All her clothes stuck to her, and she could even feel grateful for her torn skirt, which let in what little air was stirring. Halfway back to the huts, she picked up a bit of twig off the beach, and twisted it into her hair to lift the weight of it off her neck.

The defenders still held their guns, facing the jungle, but the folk on the beach were neatly lined into rows, while Father Patrick led them in prayer. Scarlet nodded to herself. Massed together, instead of strung out down the beach and hiding in huts, the cove's inhabitants looked like the town that Conner had always wanted. Too bad they were better at praying than doing something about their hardships.

Perhaps this was why Conner resented them so. Maybe he still needed pirates and escapees, rather than the good citizens of the world.

She broke into a trot to catch up, a little cooler now that her hair was off her neck, with Yeboah striding along oh his long legs beside her.

Conner marched his young captive right up to the edge of the jungle, where the shade began to devour the beach-sand. The boy struggled and pulled, but did not lose either his dignity or his courage. Scarlet stopped several strides back, her attention focused on the scene before her.

"That's you, ain't it, Aba-Wadilli?" Conner shouted. "You and your folk, what we've traded with and made welcome. It's you, and this here's your boy. We've got him, and we ain't letting him go until you come out and parlay."

Nothing in the bush moved. Conner chewed his lower lip and took a pistol from his pocket. "I know you're in there. You can hear me." he held the gun to the boy's head. The boy went still, but made no sound. Conner called out again. "Come out and tell us what you want. That's all I ask. Tell us, and we'll work it out."

Something moved, just faintly, in the shadows. Scarlet held her breath. As slowly as a great cat creeping forward, came a man. His back was straight and unbowed, skin dark bronze, and he wore no clothing but a red breechclout, but a great spray of tropical feathers crowned his head. In his hands he carried a spear, also decorated with feathers. On either side of him were two guards, with muskets leveled at Conner's face. The place in the shadows was dead quiet. Even the birds had stopped singing.

"I will speak with you," the chief said. "For the friendship we have had, and the trading. We was allies, fair and honest. Then you bring evil men into our land, to torture us and anger our land. You let them build a sword-tower. Now you ask what we want.

"Now, wait a minute…" Conner gestured with his pistol hand, and the muskets all clicked together as their triggers were pulled tight.

The chief locked eyes with Conner and the two stared for a long minute. Finally Conner said, "Just tell me what you want to bring us back to peace."

"Peace is what you want?"

Conner's eyes shown as if with unshed tears. "I swear."

"Then give us the black-robe, and put fire on his tower, and we will see."

Conner shook the boy in his grip. "And what about this one?"

The chief's eyes flicked. "My son wishes to be a man. I wish to protect my people."

"Father Patrick!" Conner bellowed. "Get yourself here!"

The good father came, black robe flapping around his ankles, sleeves rolled above the elbow, smeared with blood and sand. His face was grim. "And what trouble do you mean to start now, you heathen, and me just closing the eyes of the dead?"

Conner whipped around on the priest and knocked him to the ground, then rested a foot on the man's chest in one smooth motion, and leveled the pistol. "This man says you've been molesting his folk. I can't stand for that. Not if it damns me to hell eternal."

The good father looked nothing but confused, and Scarlet made bold enough to remark, "The world here can only be so much like the old one, Father. Now it looks like your luck has run out. A shame too, for I'd wanted to hear mass on Sunday."

The priest looked form Conner to Scarlet. "And what account must I give?"

Conner looked down at the priest, and his eyes were grim. "So you've been tormenting these folk, who owned this land before us? You've been after molesting them?"

Despite his position on the ground, the priest's chin went up. "How can you ask it of me? Doesn't the Holy Book call us to peace? You're the fellows with the muskets."

His flat rejection gave Conner pause. "You ain't been messing with the natives?"

"And why would I mess with anyone, with houses to be built and the church going up, and you folk luring my flock to sin twice and three times a day?"

Conner turned back to the chief. "Is this him? Is this the man?"

"It is his tribe."

It didn't make one bit of sense to Scarlet. She'd heard of the Spanish torturing folk to get them to convert, but it didn't seem Father Patrick's line of work. Besides, as the man said, if he wanted to make the Donnellys into churchgoers, he would have his hands full for years.

"Hey!" Sean asked, staring from face to face. "What the hell's a sword tower? Where's it at?"

Both Conner and Aba-Wadilli stared as if Sean had lost his mind, and Scarlet began to get an idea.

The chief waved his arm back in the direction of the church. "That. We have watched it built. It is a mark that you intend war."

Conner only looked confused. Scarlet asked, "You mean the church steeple?"

"We have taken in those fleeing from the black-robe tribe. When those towers are built, it means war, and people enslaved, and death for many."

Scarlet chewed on that fact, turning it over in her mind. "Conner! He means the Spanish! They have priests among 'em. They always do."

Conner looked at the priest. "You swear you ain't been trying to convert anyone? I told you not to do that."

"Only you and your brothers, for all the good it's done me."

Scarlet was watching the native chief's face. For the first time, she saw doubt, and pushed ahead with her thought. "He ain't never seen an Irish priest, Conner. All the Catholics on the mainland are Spaniards. What's the first thing they do? Put up a church! And what's the second? Enslave every native in the area, and set 'em digging for gold!"

Conner thought for a moment. "Sure it is!" He threw the pistol onto the ground. "Aba-Wadilli, them's not our people. We're on the run from 'em too. This fellow, Father Patrick..." he reached out and grabbed the priest by the shoulder, "Ain't about to catch or torture anyone. He'll mind his manners, I swear."

"He is from the same tribe..."

"Well, he is and he ain't. It's a long story. And I'd be honored, right honored, if you folk would come down on the beach and talk about it. It's too hot out here in the damn woods."

"You swear that the black-robes from the south are a different tribe? And that you do not intend war?"

Conner reached down to help Father Patrick to his feet. "Well, Father, why don't you answer them? Why don't you tell 'em how much you're willing to do to end this bloodshed?" And as he dusted the priest off, Scarlet heard him add, "And it had better be good, for I told you not to build that tower in the first place."

The priest stood looking at the natives, at their bronze skin and their nakedness and their feathers, and then clasped his hands together and said most sincerely, "I am a man driven from his homeland, and dreaming to make a place like it on the far side of the world. I don't know you, or your folk. I only mean to keep my people safe, in their bodies and their souls. We are torn apart by fighting. Let us talk together, so we can find a way to keep peace within this land."

The chief raised his spear and gave out a long, shrieking cry, then nodded to Conner in a most civilized fashion. "I will speak with Conner Donnelly, and I will speak with Conner's friend."

Conner nodded. "I'd be most happy to talk. There are too many dead folk on this beach as it is."

⌘

Branna came in to tend the wounded, and worked side by side with the native healers, cozy as cousins. The dead lay wrapped in sailcloth, ready for burying on the morrow.

Scarlet stood by Conner, pulling on her beer, waiting for him to finish talking to Father Patrick. When the good father finally nodded and went his way, she caught the front of Conner's short and pulled him around. "Was that good enough, love? All's well as ends with a drink, and you have the peace you wanted."

Conner put up a hand and pushed her away. "No thanks to you, dropping folk off here like selling sheep at a fair. And forcing my hand. Lot of dealing you did, for one broadside that leveled half my town."

Scarlet pouted, but Conner seemed not to notice. "A broadside ain't no careful thing, love, and I did finally gather what the problem was. Surely that's worth a kiss in the dark? And maybe a bit more, if you fancy it?"

Conner sighed and finally met her eyes. "I don't fancy. I ain't some wild buccaneer no more, I'm a mayor, or a king, or something. It's a sight more work than I planned."

She come in closer and pushed her hip up against him. "All the more reason to take your ease while you can."

Conner slowly shook his head and pushed her away. "No. You wanted to deal. We've dealt. I owe you, but that's all. Go find some young man, Scarlet, for I feel mighty old this night."

Conner walked back nearer the fire and began speaking with Aba-Wadilli and Scarlet stood alone, watching them.

The Shantyman came up, drink in hand. "Evening Cap'n. Will they want my voice at the burying, do you think?"

Scarlet shook her head. "It's priest-talk for this lot. They're turning lawful. Pretty soon they won't answer to the sea-gods."

"They're landsmen, after all." The Shantyman drank his beer, and looked at the fire, and finally said, "What about yourself? Do you think a mass on Sunday will clear you with the sea gods?"

"What have I to do with the sea gods? I give 'em their due."

"Aye. Aye you do, for yourself. But you cursed your ship this day, when we wouldn't fight beside you."

"That? That was no proper curse. I'm sure the sea gods understand." Scarlet stood looking at the bonfire, the Shantyman standing by her side.

"I hope you're right, Cap'n," he murmured. "I do at that."

Blood Red Sea

The *Donnybrook* descended on the little snow *Alice* like a hawk striking down from a clear blue sky. The *Alice* turned and tried to flee, but the *Donnybrook* kept bearing down, the wind strong in her sails, the blue water running under her hull like silk.

Scarlet, in her second-best coat and a feathered hat, lined her boarding party up against the starboard rail. They wore their wildest raiding clothes, tattered finery, bright India silks and odd bits of antique armor. Swords and pistols were in their hands and they shrieked vile threats and curses.

As the two ships came abreast, Scarlet ran up to the *Donnybrook*'s quarterdeck, cutlass in hand, and bellowed. "Heave your arse over, or I'll blow you down!" At her signal, Mister Bracegirdle put a canon-shot across the little ship's bow.

The *Alice*'s trembling sailors shook the wind from her sails, and she fell off, turning with the current. Pryce brought the *Donnybrook* in and they bound the *Alice* tight.

The snow's deck was nearly level to the *Donnybrook*'s. Scarlet leaped from quarterdeck to quarterdeck, the first one over. She faced a middle-aged man, whose frightened eyes

28

darted from her cutlass to her face to the curve of her breasts under her linen shirt. His hands hovered at waist height, indecisive. He was tan and fit, and his grey coat fit him well.

Scarlet leveled her sword at his midsection. "You the captain?"

His voice shook as he replied. "Yes, Captain John…"

"Well, Cap'n John, good day to you. You hove over as I said, so you've nothing much to fear. Keep doin' as I tell you and you'll sleep sound in your own bunk tonight."

Scarlet saw some form of resistance in the angle of his body and the way his fingers twitched. She looked into his eyes, then said, "You have weapons on you?"

He shook his head. "N-no."

"Take off your coat."

She accepted the coat, hefting its weight in her hand. Too light to conceal anything dangerous, but nonetheless she threw it over to the deck of the *Donnybrook*, ten feet away.

Scarlet looked into his eyes again and took a step closer, then another. When she was close enough that their bodies nearly touched, she reached over and slid a hand along the waistband of his breeches. His eyes went wide, the pupils dilating.

"Let's see… ah, here it is!" Her fingers found a pistol, tucked in along his spine. "All you fellers are alike. The same shite, over and again." She smashed the cutlass' knuckle guard against his jaw by way of punishment and checked the pistol while he was picking himself up off the deck. It was primed and loaded, but her pockets already bulged with pistols. She flipped open the priming pan of with her thumb and let the powder trickle out before tossing it after the coat.

"You might of kept that if you'd put it away sensible," she said.

He cupped his bruised face with a shaking hand. Now he was beginning to sweat. Scarlet glanced down onto the main deck, where her boarding party had herded the *Alice*'s crew towards the bow. "Who's you quartermaster?"

"It's a small ship. I serve the function."

"Very fine." Scarlet glanced down to the main deck and called "Burgess?"

"Here, Captain," called Burgess, clambering over the rail.

Scarlet turned back to Captain John. "I want your logbook, and then this man needs your manifests. Everything. The quicker we're done here the quicker we leave."

Captain John pointed to a small writing desk, set out on the quarterdeck, where a book and inkstand stood abandoned.

"That's grand. Now take Mister Burgess below and show him them manifests. And John..." Scarlet held up her sword. "Treat him like a gentleman, and I'll do the same for you."

As the man hurried away Scarlet dropped the cutlass into its scabbard and sat, going through the log. The last entry had been cut off short, the final two words being "black flag". It seemed Captain John had dropped everything and run around panicked as soon as they'd been sighted.

She began examining entries. Three days past, she found reference to a lanteen-rigged sloop the *Alice* had passed. Scarlet could not spell out the long Spanish name, but noted the position and heading. They might be able to catch that ship up as well. Then she skimmed, running a finger along each line, looking for words she knew.

Here was one. Flogging. Captain John wrote a fine hand, and she was able to make out the whole entry with effort. Two men fighting, six lashes each. Fair enough. She had to go back a month to find another flogging. This time she couldn't make out what the problem was but the punishment had been twelve.

Captain John was no means soft, but reasonable. Scarlet felt no desire to do anything drastic. She took out a pistol and descended to the main deck. Everything was going well, the *Alice*'s crew quiet, Pryce and the other pirates alert and in control. Scarlet went below.

"What've we got, Mister Burgess?"

He was smiling, checking things off on a list. "Grand, Captain. Indigo, rice, silver plate, and a case of six dozen pocket watches! Do you want us to take any stores?"

"Just fresh stuff. And some rice, not all of it. Is that a goat I hear?"

"It is. There's a chicken, too."

"Bring them over. And, let's say," she paused to consider Captain John's attempt to hide the pistol against the needs of his crew. "… half the grog. I'm going into the captain's cabin for the strongbox. Oh, and if there's a length of muslin or calico, bring that."

Captain John's cabin contained the usual bunk, desk and large sea chest, but also two cases of wine and some wheels of fine cheese. Scarlet called for someone to take them. Sanchez came and directed two of the *Alice*'s crew to do the lifting, while Scarlet went through the desk. She found letters, a miniature portrait of a dark-haired woman, writing paper, a ring of keys, which she laid out, and a half-empty bottle of scotch whiskey. The bottom drawer was locked, but a key from the ring fit.

Inside was a jumble of clothing, crammed into the spaces around the wooden strong box. Scarlet had expected the chest, but she had not expected the clothes. She began to examine the room more critically. The bunk seemed lumpy.

She went to it and pulled the coverlet back, revealing a mess of clothing, boots, a sword and several books.

Someone had unloaded the sea chest in a hurry. Scarlet found the right key, unlocked the chest, aimed a pistol and flipped the lid open.

A girl screamed, and Scarlet saw two terrified grey eyes, a tumble of ash-blonde curls and a pair of pink lips that screamed again and then began to babble in French.

"Calm down, girl, calm down." Scarlet put the pistol away. "I ain't planning to harm you."

The girl hunkered in the chest, bracing herself as if fearful that Scarlet was going to drag her out. Scarlet tried again. "*Anglaise?*"

"*Oui.*"

"You belong to Captain John?"

"*Non.* I am…" the girl concentrated on her pronunciation of the words, "working for my passage."

"You work there?" Scarlet pointed to the bunk.

The girl's cheeks went pink. She nodded.

"Where'd you book passage to?"

"Martinique to Guadeloupe. My sister is married there."

Scarlet clenched her teeth and then forced herself to relax. "You run away from your position?"

A nod. "My name is Celeste. I am a maid for Monsignor Giscard. His wife, she does not like me. She beats me. So I thought I would go to my sister."

"But this Giscard owns you, don't he? He won't let you go?"

"*Oui. Non.*" The girl's eyes filled up with tears. "You are a pirate, *non?* What will you do with me?"

"Well, I ain't going to rape you. Come on, get out 'o there. How long you been sailing, girl?"

32

"Three weeks. Are we near to Guadeloupe yet?"

"You might be, if you hadn't passed it up so long ago. This here boat is off the coast of the Caicos, three hundred miles past. Guadeloupe and Martinique are only about fourteen hours apart."

The girl's cheeks went an entirely different shade of pink, and her eyes flashed. "That... That... That... man!"

"Well, some of 'em are like that. Come along, come out of there."

The girl climbed from the chest, bringing with her a bundle of clothes. She wore a neat linen maid's dress in pale grey, with a bit of lace showing at the neck, and buckled shoes. Once she was clear, she stood looking at the deck, trying to put up her hair. Her shaking hands kept dropping the pins.

Scarlet gave her time, putting her own attention to opening the strongbox. When she found the right key and pushed the lid open she whistled. Most of what lay within were heavy gold four-escudo coins, each with a picture of the Spanish king.

The chest was almost too heavy to lift, Scarlet called up for help. When Sanchez came back down, he paused to smile at the French girl. She cringed and shivered.

"Put yer eyes back in your head, Sanchez. Take this box and put it straight into Mister Burgess' hands. No other." Scarlet clicked the lock back into place, put the keys in her pocket. A sudden thought occurred, and she turned back to Celeste. "Anything here you fancy, girl?"

Celeste went straight to the boots on the bed, reached into the left one, and pulled out a pair of gold shoe buckles. Scarlet barked a laugh. "Good work! Anything else I should know about?"

Celeste found two more bottles of liquor, another book, and a tin box of sugar candy hidden around the cabin. Scarlet tied them up with her own finds in the coverlet from the bed and hauled everything out into the passageway. "Come on, girl. My crew's coming down."

Celeste followed her down the passageway carrying her own little bundle, and climbed up into the sunlight, close as a longboat in tow, until she spotted Captain John. Then she threw down her bundle, stormed over to him and slapped him so hard he staggered backward.

The man's face drew into an angry snarl and he raised a hand to hit her back, but Pryce shoved her pistol into his cheek and said, "I told you to be still. You do as you're told."

Celeste began screaming like a fishwife, a rapid torrent of French that made Pryce turn away and blush. Everyone on the deck stared. Burgess sidled over to Scarlet and whispered, "What's she saying?"

She could barely suppress her laughter. "Mostly that he's a piss-poor bunkmate, 'n his parents didn't know each other well. Also something about the goat. Faith. And the chicken."

While Celeste entertained her crew, Scarlet watched the progress of moving the plunder. The *Donnybrook*'s big wooden cargo-crane had been set up, and the pirates were running the capstan to lift cargo directly from the *Alice*'s hold to their own deck. When the last load was hauled out and she could hear the goat bleating from the *Donnybrook*, Scarlet turned back to the *Alice*'s sailors.

"Well now, you've been robbed, and it weren't so bad. Now I make you all an offer. If you've a mind to join us, come over. You'll have free use of the ship's grog and food, a full share of plunder, and the right to vote on ship's business, according to our laws. Anyone here ready to go on the account?"

Some of the men stirred restlessly. A voice called out, "Can we have the wench?"

Celeste squeaked.

"You may not," Scarlet answered. "The girl belongs to 'erself now."

"What'll you do with her?"

Scarlet put her fists on her hips and looked back at Celeste. "Will you come along with us? Or stay here?"

Celeste looked about in confusion for a moment, then held out the gold buckles. "Take me to Guadeloupe. I will give you these."

Scarlet shook her head. "I don't run a passage ship. You come as crew or not at all."

The French girl licked her lips, nervous. Finally she stared into Scarlet's eyes and asked, "What would I do on your ship?"

"When a rope is put in your hand, you will haul. When a thing needs moved, you will carry. When the deck is dirty, you will learn to clean it."

"And that is all?"

"It should be near enough to kill you, girl, if you do it right." Scarlet could hear her crew chuckling behind her. "But we don't keep whores. You'll work on your feet."

"Then I will come with you."

"Very well." Scarlet indicated the knotted coverlet at her feet. "Start by takin' this over. And don't forget your own things."

Keeping her eyes on the pirates, Celeste gathered the two bundles and began to struggle over onto the *Donnybrook*.

"That one will be as useful as teats on a bull."

Scarlet looked at Pryce in mild surprise. "She's violent as an Irish lass. She'll do fine."

"I hope so." Pryce waved her pistol at the *Alice*'s crew. "We done here?"

Scarlet looked at the assembled men. "Let's shove off."

⌘

As the *Donnybrook* got underway, Burgess spread a blanket on the open deck and began to tally the spoils, noting everything in his big brown ledger. Scarlet gave him the keys to the strongbox, then took Celeste below and saw her issued a hammock and some proper work clothes.

"Change into these," she told the girl. "I'll send Mister Flynn down in a minute. You're to do as he tells you. He won't harm you, but he'll keep you plenty busy. What's your last name?"

"Celeste Moreau."

"You go by 'Mister Moreau' now. It's a mark of honor. You ain't a chamber maid, you're learning a trade, and the trade is piracy. You call all the crew, male and female, by 'Mister' and their last name. The officers are 'Sir'. Mister Pryce is one of the officers, and so she is 'Sir' as well."

"But she is a woman."

"She is, but bein' an officer is the more important thing. You call me 'Captain' or 'ma'am'. Mister Flynn will introduce you around and see to it that you're busy. Don't worry, you will be. There's islands ahead, which means we'll be working sail, and it seems that every bit of fish shite in the sea finds its way to our deck.

"Now, hop to. Leave your things in the hammock. We'll get you a sea chest from the next ship we plunder."

Back on deck, Burgess sat on his heels, counting the coins he had spread out before him on a blanket. When Scarlet's shadow fell on him, he looked up and said, "The trade goods, the watches and the Indigo and the silver plate, are all in the hold. I can only guess at their value until we sell them, but they're noted down. These coins should feed the crew ashore for three months, if they would be prudent. They will not, so I imagine we need six more hauls like this, if we don't want be out when the hurricanes blow."

"That's fine, then." Scarlet pointed to the half-empty whiskey bottle. "I had no chance to taste that."

Burgess handed it over, and Scarlet pulled the cork and tilted the bottle back, letting a taste of the amber liquid slide over her tongue. "Mmm. That's good. I'll have this and them other two bottles as part of my share."

"I'll mark it down."

Scarlet carried the bottles into her cabin, unloaded her pockets and checked the priming of each pistol before putting it away. She unbuckled her sword belt, then picked up the shirt she had been making and pulled herself up onto the wide sill of the aft cabin window to catch the light.

She had been working for nearly an hour when someone knocked at the door. "Come in."

It was Celeste. She looked magnificently out of place in sailor's work clothes, and stared at the deck in shame of her bare legs, but gamely repeated, "Mister Pryce's compliments, and would you please come up to the *quatre-deck*?"

"Tell Mister Pryce I'll be there directly." Celeste nodded and the door closed. Scarlet put her attention back to her sewing, took two more stitches to finish the seam, tied off the thread and snapped the loose end. She put the shirt away, buckled on her sword, and picked up a brace of pistols. Then she headed up to the quarterdeck.

"Anything of interest?"

Pryce nodded ahead. "According too the charts we're coming to a right maze of narrow channels and islets. I wanted to know if you had thoughts."

Before Scarlet could answer, a voice called out from the bow, "Seven fathoms! Seven fathoms and sand bottom!"

"Is it level?" Scarlet asked.

"No. I'm seeing all kinds of things. Sand, coral… Is it worth it to go on?"

Scarlet weighted the value of a known target against the danger to her ship's bottom.

The leadsman in the bow called out again, "Two fathoms, coral!"

"What do you figger? Bear away west-nor'west and we'll hang about the Maya Passage?"

Pryce was just opening her mouth to reply when the lookout called down. "Ship! Sixty degrees starboard! A lanteen-rigged sloop!"

Scarlet smiled a Pryce, then called back, "How's she bearing?"

The lookout took a while to reply. "She's bumbling about… Don't seem to like these currents. Changing tack." Along pause, and then he called down, "Heading looks to be west-nor'west."

Pryce grinned. "A little more canvas and we can swing around that island ahead and meet them coming out."

"Just my thought. More canvas, Mister Flynn. And prepare to come about."

Pryce prepared the maneuver, and when the crew had drawn the *Donnybrook*'s vast mainsail to its full height, and were resting and panting, Scarlet called them together and spoke to them.

"That last haul was dead perfect. We scared the heart out of 'em, and stayed calm doing it. Let's have that again. I want every cannon and pistol loaded, every sword ready. The more they think we're willing to fight, the less we'll have to. It's hurricane season upon us. Let's fill the *Donny*'s hold with treasure for it."

The crew cheered and scrambled to their places. Celeste came to Scarlet and asked, "What am I to do in this ship's battle?"

"We took a pistol in that last haul. Tell Mister Burgess I said to give it to you. William or Mister Bracegirdle will show you how to load and fire it. When we pull beside that little sloop out there, you just pretend that the man who used you so ill is on it, and give him what for. Just don't kill anyone."

"*Oui!*"

Scarlet stepped back to her cabin for another brace of pistols and paused to tie her hair up. The day was getting very warm, and the breeze falling off. She hoped they would have enough wind to take the little sloop by dinnertime.

As they came around the island, Pryce and Flynn called out to each other time and again, adjusting the rudder and the sails to best take advantage of the fading breeze. Scarlet worked off her impatience by hauling with the rest, digging her boot heels into the deck and straining until her belly hurt.

"Captain, can you come?" Pryce was straining to look ahead. Scarlet trotted up the gantry to stand beside her.

"We're in position, ma'am, but the wind's fading fast. Request permission to head in along the north side of the island. I think we can catch them up before dusk. It'd be no fun to rattle around all night, looking for 'em in the dark."

Scarlet called forward. "How's the bottom?"

"Sand, coral and broken shells, mixed. Four fathoms."

"We can get purchase on that, if we lose the wind entire and have to drop anchor. You have my permission, Pryce." Scarlet called forward to the main deck. "Flynn, ready to drop anchor."

"Ready, Cap'n!"

Slowly, slowly. The *Donnybrook* was moving at a walking pace. The ship's cook called them to dinner, and Scarlet ate her goat meat and rice while sitting by the bow, sighting along the coast. The shadow of the island fell long across the sea.

Something. Scarlet blinked into the growing darkness. Was it possible that the shape she saw ahead was their prey? "Sunny Jim," she called to the man eating his dinner amidships. "Is that the ship? Give me your eyes. What see you?"

A long pause. "It's the ship." He paused, standing on his toes, then ran a few steps up the ratlines. "That's the one. But there are others, too. War canoes, Cap'n. Many of 'em."

"What are they doing? You sure they ain't just coming out to trade?"

Sunny Jim shook his head, slowly. "That don't look like a trading party to me."

Scarlet caught her breath. Something was off, natives didn't attack unless sorely pressed. This shouldn't be happening. She strained to see through the dusk. She could just make out the rough outlines of moving things. But Sunny Jim had eyes that no one doubted.

The thudding noise of a small cannon echoed over the water, followed by scattered reports of muskets. "They're swarming all over it," Sunny Jim called down.

Natives attacking a ship. Such a thing might mean madness, or it might mean war. Scarlet took a deep breath and began to work her way back along the deck, urging the crew to be quiet. "Those natives may not have seen us. If they haven't let's not draw attention."

The ship fell silent, the only noise the soft groaning of her timbers. Scarlet felt her way back to Pryce, felt the wind on her cheek, hardly more than a whisper, and called softly up, "Can you turn her?"

"No. We're drifting with the current."

With no wind to drive them, they were helpless, either to fight or to run away. Scarlet watched their progress. The current was carrying them slowly toward the equally-becalmed sloop and the vast number of violent natives. It was too strong for the longboat to tow them against. "Loose the anchor, then."

The anchor fell with a soft 'plash' and the ship drifted to a stop.

Someone on the other ship began to scream.

For a long time Scarlet and her crew stood, silent, looking out across the water. The screaming turned to hysterical pleading, then another voice joined it. Some shrieks were cut off short, but most went on and on, voices full of terror and pain.

Scarlet shook herself out of her horror. She straightened her shoulders and pitched her voice to carry. "Come on. This ain't the first time we faced somethin' dangerous. Let's get to work. Rig to repel boarders. No lights. They likely ain't seen us, and I mean to keep it that way."

She found Bracegirdle in the dark, and spoke to him

in a low, firm voice. "Load all the cannon with grape shot." A particularly tortured voice rose up, but she kept speaking over it. "Unship the front wheels on the guns, so they point downward. A dose of canon fire will teach these bastards some respect."

Then she moved among the crew, giving instructions. "Fetch a keg of powder, kegs of shot, and all the paper cartridges up on deck." "Make sure every musket and pistol on this boat is loaded and handy." "Heave some water buckets up here in case of fire." "No lights. We will not make ourselves a target." "Be sure everyone has a sword or an axe." "Get both the boathooks out on deck. We can use them as weapons." "Spread out, damn you. Pick a piece of railing and hold it."

Across the water the terrible noises went on. Scarlet concentrated on getting the *Donnybrook*'s work groups together, keeping them active, keeping them focused on the possible attack. "We don't know they've even seen us," she repeated over and over. "That little sloop ain't half our size, and ain't well armed." "Of course they're getting tore up, they can't even tack proper."

The rising half-moon gave some light and she found the Shantyman. "Where's my wind?"

"Strung out between the Lesser Antilles and Donnelly's cove. You used it all."

"Get me more."

"With all due respect, Cap'n, it ain't as easy as that."

"Climb up top and work on it."

He bent over a keg on deck, filled one of his many pouches with gunpowder, and began to climb.

At last, Scarlet could think of no more tasks for her people. They sat quietly in the dark, each stationed at a section of railing, listening to the fading voices from the other ship. A fire flared on the beach. A drum began. Scarlet realized she was reciting the rosary under her breath.

They sat long in the dark, waiting. The moon went up in the sky and the fire on the beach burned down. Scarlet stationed herself on the landward side, amidships. She settled in and waited, looking out across the dark water. How she hoped that they had not been spotted, that all the preparations had been useless, that dawn would bring wind and they could sail away from here.

A voice shrieked, not five feet from her left ear, and Scarlet started to her feet. She had been dozing. She shook herself and raised her pistol. Wooden canoes bumped against the *Donnybrook*'s side, and weird forms clambered up over her railing. Their forms where roughly human, their heads bulged in bizarre shapes. Worst of all were their eyes, huge glowing things that stared sightlessly. Scarlet found a pair of those eyes, aimed right between them and pulled the trigger.

The priming pan flared in the darkness and then the pistol barked. The thing shrieked and fell with a splash. Two more came up behind it. Pistols flashed to left and right. Scarlet dropped her gun and drew two more. The left one didn't fire when she pulled the trigger, and the monster she was aiming at got one leg over the rail before the man to Scarlet's left struck it in the neck with an axe and it fell back. She gave the fouled pistol one more try as she drew her last one and fired again, then dropped both guns and drew her sword.

She hacked, and felt a grim satisfaction when something under the sword broke and shrieked. Nothing else followed it. "Everyone all right?" Scarlet bellowed.

"Help. Need some help." For'd.

Scarlet ran up by the bow. One of the things had made the deck. Flynn and two other pirates, holding axes and swords surrounded it, too fearful to strike. As Scarlet approached, the creature stabbed with something long and thin, then threw itself forward, carrying Flynn to the deck. Scarlet heard grunting and Flynn's screech. She went to her knees beside the struggling figures, felt until she found the head of the creature and pounded down with the hilt of her sword.

It turned on her with its teeth, ripping at her hand. She whipped at it with the sword and it rolled away, scrambled onto all fours, and leaped off into the water. Scarlet looked after it, trying to control her shaking knees.

One of the others helped Flynn to his feet. He was clutching his torn throat. "What the bloody hell was that?" he whispered.

Scarlet gritted her teeth. "They're things as die when we shoot them. Get below and have Branna wrap that up. You two, back to your stations." She called out into the ship. "Who's reloading?"

"I am!" William's voice piped up from the center of the ship.

"All empty pistols to center! Burgess, Moreau, to center and load pistols! Mister Bracegirdle, can you sight the cannons?"

"No ma'am! The canoes are too small and movin' too fast."

A voice called out from the stern. "What are those things, Captain?"

Sunny Jim chimed in, "They ain't human!"

Someone moaned.

"Stop it!" Scarlet shouted. "Don't be children afeared of the dark! These things die! That's all we need. Keep killing 'em and they'll go."

"They're *sluaghs*, monsters."

"Shut your gob, Sunny Jim, or I will have it shut."

Someone shouted from the seaward side, and a gun went off amidships. Scarlet barked "Hold your places! Port side, are you attacked?"

"Aye, they're… Good god, what are they?"

"Never mind. Shoot."

It took every bit of strength Scarlet had to keep from running over to help on the port side, but she knew she must set an example by holding her position. She compromised by demanding, "Are you holding? Are you holding?"

She heard gunfire, the thunk of swords against wood, against bodies. Finally she could stand it no more and turned. She was just in time to see one of the creatures scramble past the crew. Once again, when the thing made the deck, the pirates fell back before it in superstitious terror. In the moonlight Scarlet had only the vaguest impression of a body covered with shaggy hair, a bizarrely shaped head and those enormous, staring white eyes.

She didn't give herself time to think, but stepped forward and chopped with the cutlass. Blood squirted out on the deck, but the thing still struggled. "Help me," Scarlet ordered, and others came in and finished it off.

They were paying for the *Donnybrook's* design. Thanks to her shallow draft the main deck didn't sit high. And her railing, unlike a warship, was openwork instead of solid panels. The creatures, coming in on their canoes, could reach up catch the edge of the deck and pull themselves up.

"Mister Yeboah," Scarlet called into the darkness. "Get a boathook. When you see these bastards coming for the sides, knock 'em off, into the water. Pray God they don't know how to swim."

The next wave was upon them. Scarlet caught up a pistol, fired, then hacked with the sword. Her arm was beginning to tire. This time they came on both sides. One of her crew was dragged into the water, screaming. The pirates were frightened. More and more, Scarlet heard prayers among the curses and grunts of effort.

Scarlet's right hand was growing numb. She kept finding a way to raise her arm and cut, again and again. The flashes of gunfire came seldom now. It simply took too much time to load a pistol. Scarlet thought to herself. "If we get out of this alive, we need more pistols."

She kept shouting words of encouragement to the crew. They were brave enough against things they understood, but these monsters in the dark terrified them. She knew the only thing that kept them fighting was the fact that there was no place to run to.

For a while, the ship was quiet. Scarlet called up into the rigging, "Shantyman, where's my wind?"

"It's far above, playin' with the clouds."

"Call it down!"

"I've promised it every sweet thing I can think of, Captain."

"I have two good bottle of Scotch whisky in my cabin. Promise that as well."

Pryce's voice rang out, "May I have them, Captain, if I blow into the sails hard enough?" It drew a ragged few laughs.

Scarlet smiled and looked around, making sure that her perimeter was still properly manned. Her shoulder ached. Her hand cramped. Then her whole right arm began to shake uncontrollably. Her cutlass clattered to the deck, and she bent, pressing the arm against her thigh, pounding on it with the fist of other hand.

"Are you all right Cap'n?" asked Bracegirdle.

"Branna. See if Branna can come."

The arm felt like some alien thing. She could not make it stop trembling, and the last two fingers were numb. Scarlet fought her hand into a fist and pounded her leg, trying to bring the feeling back.

She was aware of a thud against the side of the ship, and then the sound of scrabbling nails on wood. Before she could shout a warning, more of the creatures were coming over the side. The first one knocked her sprawling, and then Bracegirdle was grappling with another one, and Scarlet was hit, hard, on the side of the body, and struggled over onto her back to grapple with the monster on top of her.

This close it stank, and the hanging fur around its shoulders shut out the moonlight. Scarlet kicked and bit while her right arm guarded her throat and her left hand groped at the small of her back for a knife. The weight of the monster pressed her down, but finally her reaching fingers found the blade and pulled it free. Then she was stabbing in the dark, off-handed, while the thing tore at her with its teeth and all she could see was those eyes, those unnatural staring eyes.

A pistol blasted above her, and the thing groaned and rolled away. At the next blast, Scarlet saw William's terrified face in the brief flash of light, and his hands holding the weapon in a clumsy, two-handed grip.

Scarlet tried to get to her feet, slipped in the blood on the deck, and crawled away from the rail. She felt stunned. Her body didn't move properly. William caught her by her damaged shoulder and pulled. She gritted her teeth and did her best to help.

A clutch of wounded huddled in the center of the ship. There were too many. Scarlet looked along the rail. They were spread so thin! If the whole of the crew, firing muskets and pistols, had not been able to drive the creatures away, how could they keep holding out when their numbers had been cut in half?

Something scrabbled at the side of the ship and the pirates grouped wearily to beat it off. Scarlet staggered to her feet, then stood helpless, watching. She'd dropped her knife, her cutlass lay somewhere along the railing. She was not skilled with her off hand, and the aching, shaking right arm made even focusing her mind difficult.

Another lull in the fighting. Every move made by the crew revealed how exhausted they were. Scarlet tried to think of something inspiring to say, but the words rattled around in her brain, useless.

They needed a new plan. Her tired brain spun. The attacks had come from port and starboard, and one from near the bow. The creatures hadn't tried to come up over the stern. The quarterdeck stood six feet above the main deck, accommodating the captain's cabin, and they hadn't managed to scale the extra height. If she could get all the crew crammed onto the quarterdeck, the monsters would have to climb to the deck and then come up the gangway.

Retreating to the quarterdeck would mean abandoning the rest of the ship, with all its weapons and stores, a truly last resort. But a last resort was better than no resort at all. Scarlet began trying to calculate how to get as many weapons as possible onto the quarterdeck.

She heard the thunk of a canoe against the ship, and turned her head, listening for the sound of scrabbling on the railings. But instead, what reached her ears was the sound of breaking glass.

The only glass on the *Donnybrook* was the aft cabin window.

She threw herself at the cabin doors and held her bodyweight against them, just as they started to open. At first she could only scream "Help!" over and over in a too-high voice. Then she found her captain's voice and bellowed, "Mister Yeboah to aft cabin door! Need help to repel boarders at aft cabin!"

More bodies fell in beside hers and they held the doors against the creatures. Scarlet dared to step back and think. They must either do something decisive or die, and she didn't want to die yet.

A thought finally swam into her exhausted brain, and she called out, "Bracegirdle, re-ship them wheels and haul me a canon to fire on this door!"

"Aye, Cap'n!" Scarlet heard the scraping and dragging as Bracegirdle's gunners hauled a huge brass cannon across the deck. Scarlet managed to pant, "Closer!" Then she signaled for the others to fall back. When she tried to step back herself, she stumbled over a spent pistol and fell.

The door smashed open and Bracegirdle shouted, "Fire!"

The gunner pulled the firing cord, the hammer fell, and Scarlet saw the priming powder flash in the dark. Monstrous shapes filled the cabin, filled the doorway. No sound. Scarlet waited for the deep thud of the cannon's main charge going off, but it seemed the big gun had hung fire. The monsters came on.

Then the cannon erupted. Fire blazed out the muzzle and dozens of pieces of grape-sized lead shot tore apart the door, the bulkhead, and everything else before them. A few heartbeats later, a second cannon blasted into the cabin, tearing up anything that remained alive inside.

A vast quiet settled.

Scarlet struggled to her feet, picked up a fallen axe with her left hand, and dragged herself to the open door of her cabin. Everything inside was in ruins. A thin red mist hung in the air and a dozen forms lay about. One raised a hand, and Scarlet raised the axe in answer, but the hand fell back, and Scarlet dropped the axe at her own feet.

It occurred to her that she was able to see, and she looked up at the sky to glimpse streaks of rosy light. They had fought all night. Scarlet caught movement out the broken stern window and saw six or eight war canoes paddling away.

She stood, staring about at random objects, panting, unable to catch her breath. All around her was ruin: wood splinters, dropped and broken weapons, splashes of blood, bodies.

"Will you look at that?"

Scarlet staggered over to see. A small group was clustered around one of the bodies on the deck. It was a man, an ordinary man, with a great deal of mud and feathers in his hair, and wild war paint resembling enormous eyes engulfing his own. He wore a shaggy goat-skin cape, and under that breeches and a filthy, tattered linen vest, with only one button remaining.

"Why?" was all she could think to ask.

"Shipwrecked?" Bracegirdle offered.

"Marooned?"

"Escaped slaves?"

"This one's a native," Pryce said, looking at another body. "There ain't just one explanation here."

Scarlet kicked the foot of the corpse. "Get these things overboard, before they start to stink. Clean up this mess. And Bracegirdle, for God's sake, get them guns lashed down. We don't need loose cannon rolling about the deck. I need to..." she started to step into her cabin to get the crew list, but the devastation turned her stomach, and she had to close her eyes.

She looked up into the rigging and shouted, "Shantyman, where's my wind?"

"Just commin' now, your ladyship." As if on signal, a breeze picked up a lock of Scarlet's hair and ruffled the *Donny*'s sails.

Scarlet sighed. "Pryce, the wheel. Flynn, weigh anchor." She titled back her head and called into the rigging again, "Shantyman get down here and call the list. We need to know who's living, dead or missing."

People struggled slowly about, starting their tasks. Scarlet saw her cutlass, bloodied and abandoned on the deck. She walked slowly over and bent to pick it up. But she couldn't seem to stop going down, or else the deck came up to meet her. It didn't matter. The wooden planks under her cheek were suddenly quite comfortable, and she closed her eyes.

Up Shot

Scarlet bolted awake, gasping for air, and was pressed back down onto the bunk. Something restrained her right arm. She struck out blindly with her left.

"There now, none o' that!" Branna's firm, calming voice soothed her. "We've had a rough night, and you rougher than many. Here, drink this." She held up a cup, and Scarlet swallowed.

She gagged immediately. "What in the name of Christ is that?"

"It is grog, among other things. Finish it."

Scarlet tried to get up again, and Branna pushed her down, not so gently this time. "Before you go climbing about this ship, I've something to show you. Don't make that face with me. You'll see it, sure, and think on it, before you make another move."

Scarlet lay still while Branna sat beside her and undid bandages covering her right arm and hand. The bite marks on her hand were raw and weeping, and she was black from fingers to shoulder. It looked like the arm of a corpse, not anything that should be attached to her. Scarlet held herself very still, and when she could speak asked, "Will I die?"

Branna frowned and poured honey onto the bite marks, then began to bandage again. "You may, if the hand starts to rot. It hasn't yet. The arm's not as bad as it looks. It's bruising, not poisoned blood. But you are in danger, and you need to act it. Eat what I tell you, drink what I tell you, and lay down in your bunk when I tell you to do it."

"I will." Scarlet pushed her fear away and looked out the open door. "How long have I been asleep?"

Branna slapped her, and when Scarlet's startled eyes focused on her face, held up a knife. "This. For you. If you don't behave." She laid the blade on Scarlet's bandaged wrist. "Here, if you are foolish and I am wise and catch it soon." She moved the blade to Scarlet's shoulder. "Here if you are just a little more foolish, or I less wise." She dropped the knife onto the table. "Or, we can sew you into your hammock and bury you."

Scarlet felt the fear welling up again, but this time she did not push it quite all the way down. She looked into Branna's eyes, raised the cup to her lips, and drank.

Branna accepted her surrender, and began to move around the cabin again. "I'll tie this up, and you keep it so. It will hurt. If it stops hurting, tell me. If the hand goes cold, even for a moment, tell me."

"I will."

"It will be a bad day for you all round." She tied a knot in the bandage, and patted Scarlet on the shoulder. "You've been asleep nine hours. It's four o'clock in the afternoon."

Scarlet nodded, rose to her feet, and nearly sank back onto the bunk. Her arm ached and throbbed in a way nothing ever had before. She needed every bit of strength she possessed to straighten her back and walk steady. Climbing the ladder to the main deck was like conquering a mountain. Her eyes went up as soon as she was on deck, but the sails were furled, the quarterdeck empty. Her feet recognized the movements of a ship at anchor.

The edges of her vision were starting to go black, so she found an equipment locker and sat. The deck was clear, except for blood, and a few people scrubbed at that. The aft cabin doors had been blown off. Her cabin. Her home. She looked at it and breathed, waiting to find the strength to get up and go in.

"Captain."

She turned. Pryce, Burgess and the Shantyman stood together. She nodded and asked, "Report?"

Pryce spoke first. "We're standing one hour out. Crew is resting in shifts. Ship's taking water, but the pumps are keeping up. Mister McNamara has done some work on her stern, and says that she can be made sound with reasonable effort."

"She's not sound now?"

"No. McNamara says good enough for fair sailing. I'll send him in a bit to give a full report."

"Very well. Anything else? All right then, Mister Burgess."

Burges stepped forward, fiddling with his glasses. "Half the crew are wounded. Ten cases are considered serious, and confined to hammocks." His eyes strayed to Scarlet's bandaged arm. "We lack the timber to do repairs at sea. We are short on ironwork. We are low on small shot. I had to put the rice overboard. It was wet with seawater and bursting the barrels."

"How's the aft cabin?"

"It's… We've taken the bodies out. Most of them." He took his glasses off, then put them on again. "Most of the parts of them. We have a canvas cover ready for the aft window, but we're leaving it open for now to get the… To get the smell out."

Scarlet felt her jaw tensing up, but managed to keep all expression off her face. "Very good, Mister Burgess. Shantyman, why are you here?"

"You asked me to call the list, Cap'n, as I have it in memory. I have done so and am come t' report."

"Tell me."

"King, Ward, O'Shea, Hogan and Janzoon lie in their hammocks, ready for burial. Contee and Mister Flynn are missing."

"What do you mean, missing?"

"They do not answer the call, and they are not among the dead."

"Is there any chance…"

Pryce stepped forward. "They were not captured. The… the natives took no captives, we're sure of that."

"Flynn can't be gone. I told him to raise the anchor. I remember doing it."

Pryce put a hand on Scarlet's good shoulder. "He didn't use to do that work himself. He told Jimmy, and Jimmy led the crew at the capstan."

"In the water?"

"There were sharks."

"Ah." Scarlet looked at the deck. "Very well then. We'll have the service at sunset. Mister Janzoon was Protestant, was he not? Pryce, can you read the service for that?"

"I'd be honored, Captain."

"And Contee, he worshiped some pagan gods?"

The Shantyman nodded. "He had a mask and some little clay poppets."

"Can you speak at the service?"

"I will do my best."

Scarlet nodded. "I'll read the Catholic prayer, as usual."

The others murmured assent. Scarlet gave them a moment, then spoke briskly. "Shantyman, you go look at them things and try to do a square job for Contee. Pryce, find a prayer-book. Then I want you to look at the charts and think of where we can get to work again. Them ships ain't going to rob themselves, and we need timber, iron, powder and shot. Hop to. Burgess, you stay. I need to talk to you."

The Shantyman made an effort to hang about, but Scarlet shooed him away. As he backed off, she looked around. She wanted the privacy of her cabin, but if it was still wrecked, it would not set the proper tone. The deck was not crowded, so she reckoned they had as much privacy as they were like to get on a sixty-five foot deck. She patted the edge of the storage locker. Burgess sat down beside her.

"Do we have any beer on board?"

"There's a barrel or two."

"Good. We need that up on deck for after the service. By rights we should wake the fallen tonight, and hold the service at dawn, but they won't keep in this heat. I want beer, though, not spirits. We have things to discuss. One of them is you."

"Me, Captain?"

Scarlet rubbed at her bandaged arm. "You're the best quartermaster in the Carib, Burgess, but you'll never make a sailor. Pryce is a sailor. The *Donny* needs her. I mean to put her up for second in command. You'll stay quartermaster, and keep your pay. But you'll answer to two women in the running of this ship." She paused. "If you can't do it, I'll understand."

Burgess took off his glasses and wiped his eyes. "Thank you Captain. I'm not a good second, and I know it. It will be a pleasure to turn the responsibility over to Pryce."

"It don't bother you?"

"No. Only..." he nodded at her arm. "It is because of that?"

Scarlet looked up at the sky. "It's never an ill thing, to have the affairs of the ship in order. Now get me a drink of water, my throat is parched. And help me to my cabin. I need to see the damage."

The cabin was dim, for the canvas cover flapped like draperies above the broken window. Bits of flesh and bone stuck to the bulkheads, and the deck was red. Scarlet's oak desk had been ripped to flinders. She opened a drawer, and found a piece of grape-shot lodged in the logbook. Her pewter inkwell was smashed, and ink dripped over everything. Charts ruined. The sextant case was damaged. She would need to examine the sextant later. She found some relief in the bottom drawer. Both bottles of whiskey had survived.

As she closed the drawer her arm began to throb. Her bunk stood nearby and, being out of line of the door, had not been damaged, only splashed with gore. She dragged the bloody blankets off and sat down heavily. "Burgess," she said, and paused, short of breath. "Get crew in here to clean this."

"I will." He did not move.

"And the pistols. I keep meaning to ask that. Have all the pistols been cleaned? I can't clean mine just now."

"I have your pistols safe in my cabin." He stood staring. "Captain, you might want to lay down. You're white as a boiled egg."

Scarlet could feel herself breaking out in a stinking sweat. Animal instinct told her to chase Burgess from the room and curl up in pain. She remembered the knife, said, "Get Branna," and fell back onto the bunk.

Scarlet's hearing seemed unnaturally sharp, for she could hear every step of Burgess running across the deck, every thud of his buckled shoes on the ladder. When Branna came in at the door, she smiled and said, "I called you."

"An amazing truth." Branna began to unwind the bandages. "Is the hand cold?"

"I don't know." Scarlet was thinking about her heart, the feel of it moving in her chest. With every beat, her arm throbbed. Everything else seemed a hundred leagues away.

Branna touched Scarlet's face and turned to Burgess. "Get me some rum, a lot of rum, and bring some women in here."

Branna ripped Scarlet's shirt off and cut off her skirt with a knife. When the rum came she broke the bottle open, poured the contents over Scarlet's body and commanded, "Fan her. Fan her hard."

Four or five women began to flap aprons, skirt hems or bits of cloth. Scarlet gasped and tried to push them away. The rum and the fanned breeze brought an unbearable chill, and whenever she began to warm up, even a little, Branna poured on more rum and the cold came back. Her teeth chattered. "Stop. Please stop. I'm so cold."

Branna smoothed Scarlet's hair back. "No you're not, darling. You're burning up with fever, and us trying to save you." She peered at the torn hand, rubbed the arm, and felt Scarlet's face and throat again. "Dark Maire, go to my cabin and fetch the green bottle with the willow bark that's soaking in it. And my good knife."

Scarlet cried out and tried to sit up. "Don't cut off my hand."

"Can you move it?"

The sudden surge of energy brought by terror cleared Scarlet's head, and she clutched her fingers into a fist.

"I can't see," Branna muttered, looking over the blackened limb. "It's too bruised, I can see nothing." She bent and smelled the wound carefully, all over, like a hound.

"Madame Branna, may I have a word?" The Shantyman's low, liquid voice purred through the cabin.

His answer was a thrown bottle and the command, "Out of here, you feckless eejit."

"Perhaps the Cap'n should come out o' there? What with all the malevolent ghosts?"

"What are you talking, man?"

"If your callin' don't lead you to see spirits, mine does. I've been hearing their cries all through the day, and me not strong enough to chase them off. Come out o' there, love, and bring the patient with you."

Branna looked warily into the cabin's corners and nodded, and the next thing Scarlet knew the straw mattress was being lifted and carried. Someone threw a bit of cloth over her, and then she was out in the clean air, and it seemed she could breathe for the first time in a while. "That's better," she gasped.

The Shantyman paced around Scarlet's guard of women. "Cap'n," he called over their shoulders. "I tried to tell you, quiet. There's an angry presence about. It seems centered upon you."

Scarlet felt the crew tense up without even lifting her head, so she answered back easily. "It should be. I led the ship what chased them bastards off. You wait then, Shantyman. I know how to be rid of a ghost. In a day or

59

two." She paused to breathe. "When I'm back up, I'll lead you in there, and we'll finish cleaning out the ship. Hang some canvas over that doorway in the meantime, so our guests don't catch a chill."

The crew chuckled and went back to work. Scarlet sighed and let someone tuck a blanket around her. She wanted to rest and sleep, but a captain took care of the ship, and her ship needed taking care of at the moment. "Branna," she asked, low. "Are we ready for the service?"

"I'm just after sewing a few of Flynn's things into his hammock. Here, drink." She poured out a cup full of liquid the color of weak tea. Scarlet tried to gulp it down without tasting it, and did not quite succeed.

"Carry me below. Someone will have to help me dress. Better send the Shantyman to my cabin. I need my best coat."

Branna stared at her in disbelief. "You don't mean to stand up and read?"

"I do. There has never been a man or woman lost on this ship that I ain't stood for the prayer."

"Are you daft?"

"Not quite. Rig me a place on the deck to fall into. I'll rest when the service is over. But I need to be on deck to call a ship's meeting, and put some matters to the crew." Scarlet locked eyes with Branna. "We need this."

Branna dropped her gaze and nodded. "I'll find you a dress to wear."

Scarlet closed her eyes and lay back. "Tell the Shantyman to look in my sea chest. I've just finished a shirt for Yeboah. He should have it. And bring me water. I need to get this taste out of my mouth."

Whatever she Branna had given her, it seemed to take the pain away. She dutifully ate mush, and drank a mug of water, then permitted Dark Maire to button her into a linen skirt and bodice. As the sun touched the horizon, she found the strength to stand with the crew and faced the line of bodies, each sewn into the hammock they had slept in during life. The two empty ones seemed so pitiful.

Scarlet had spoke of reading, but she had memorized all the prayers for the dead long ago. She held the book in her hand, and while she recited, she held the memory of those lost. The image of Flynn's smiling face made it hard to speak. She gasped and forced her throat to relax.

Pryce and the Shantyman spoke their pieces bravely, and then silence fell. The weighted bodies splashed into the water, one after the other. The crew repeated "Amen." Scarlet raised her voice and said to the assembled crew, "Our friends lived free, and died free. No more can anyone ask. Amen."

Burgess moved to open the barrels of beer.

Branna had used coils of rope and blankets to construct a sort of throne, and Scarlet eased herself down. She was as exhausted as if she'd spent a full day hauling sail.

Mister Cahill brought food out on deck, and the toasts went round. Scarlet raised her mug, over and over, but scarcely drank. She was eager only to say her piece and sleep. But the tales needed to be told. She waited until the crew was speaking of the bravery of the fallen, then struggled to her feet and raised her tankard.

"Our fellows were brave, 'tis true, but bravery is found among the living as well." The crew raised mugs and drank again. Scarlet swayed, but kept her feet. "This crew is the best amongst the islands. We have stood our ground and defeated our enemies yet again. But within a brave crew, there are those who are stronger and braver still." The crew looked expectant. "I give you, our own navigator, Charity Pryce!"

That brought a rowdy cheer, and an enthusiastic draining of mugs. Scarlet waited while they were refilled, feeling her knees shake and the sick sweat break out on her body again. "I think this woman's skill, bravery, and steadfast nature is due reward." She couldn't speak as loudly as she liked. She couldn't get enough breath. "I put her up for Second in Command, in place of Mister Burgess, who has said he is willing." Her eyesight was tunneling again. She rushed on. "Vote to be taken by the ship's company."

With that she sank down onto the seat prepared for her. The crew went quiet. She panted, found her captain's voice again, and commanded, "Mister Burgess, take the vote."

Scarlet looked into Branna's grey eyes and saw the deep circles under them. "I'm sorry. Don't mean to keep you from your rest."

"It's nothing." Branna stripped off the coat draped over Scarlet's shoulders. Scarlet thought she heard a vote of "nay" and tried to see past Branna, but the healer was as completely in the way as it was possible to be. As she tried to see or hear, Branna pressed another cup of vile fluid into her hand. Scarlet closed her eyes and drank. Branna fussed, wiping her down with more rum, until Scarlet shivered.

She heard Branna and the Shantyman talking, as if from far away.

"It's not the hand. The hand's clean, no smell and no pus. It's almost as if it's not her arm at all."

"It's them spirits, ma'am. They want to hurt her, though I don't know why just herself, and not the rest."

"Branna," Scarlet whispered. "If I die, it weren't your fault."

"Don't speak so."

Scarlet could feel a vast spirit moving around her, moaning in her ears. She wanted to fight it, but it was so much bigger than she. Odd, the Shantyman had said "ghosts". She didn't feel ghosts, only a infinite presence, vast and old as the ocean. It weighed on her, smothering her, parching her throat.

Burgess knelt beside her, looking into her face in his worried way. "The vote is taken, Captain."

Scarlet nodded. "Send someone to get them bottles of good whiskey out of my desk. Bottom left drawer. We'll toast Pryce's new position."

"The vote was 'nay'. Twenty seven to twenty five."

"What?" Scarlet's eyes crawled onto Burgess. "What do you mean 'nay'? Are they fools entire?"

The Shantyman dropped down on her other side, cross-legged on the deck. "They did not seem to feel that a change o' leadership boded well for your health, Captain. Looking at ye, they may have the right of it."

"God damn them." She tried to see past all the hovering officers, and shouted to the ship in general, "God damn you all to Hell. Do you know what it cost me to stand and call that vote?"

"They did not." Branna was staring into her eyes.

Scarlet lay gasping, her mind wheeling in slow angry circles. "Shantyman, last night, yesterday, when the native attacked. Did you ever promise them bottles of whiskey to the sea gods?"

"I've promised that, and a great sayin' of prayers, and a year off the end of me own life. Weren't them bottles broke by the cannons?"

"They were not. Get them damn things out of my desk and pour them over the side. *That* for any sailor on this boat who don't see sense. And get me below. I'm tired of laying about on deck like a coil of rope." She turned an angry eye on Burgess. "Did you have my cabin cleaned?"

"Not yet, Captain."

"I expect to be back in there noon tomorrow." The effect was somewhat diminished when she was forced to stop talking and gasp for air.

"Ay, Captain."

Mister Yeboah picked her up in his arms like a doll and carried her below to Branna's cabin. Scarlet could hear the crew resume toasting the dead, more solemnly now, but the sound didn't keep her awake long.

She awoke in the depths of night, sweating and in pain yet again. Around her the ship swayed and creaked. She could hear Branna's soft, regular breathing. Quietly, Scarlet fought her way out of the bodice, easier because the arm and side had been split to accommodate her bandages, and then out of the skirt. Cooler, wearing just her shift, she lay, yearning for a breeze. The roots of her hair felt dirty and clogged with sweat.

She found the rum bottle and cloth on the table by feel, and sponged herself off. For the first time, the liquid felt soothing, not frigid. She celebrated by tipping the bottle back and having a few swallows. It raised her temperature again, but eased her back to sleep.

Morning brought Pryce's whisper. "Captain, are you well?"

"Better." Scarlet lay looking up at the deck beams, listening to Branna's breathing, enjoying the faint shaft of light that filtered down the passageway. "What's about?"

"Sail on the horizon. I should dearly like to know if you think we should run or fight."

"What is it?"

"Sunny Jim thinks a large fluyt or some sort of West India merchant."

She lay panting and thinking for a moment. "How's the weather?"

"Clouding a little to the southeast. Bracegirdle says it may rain."

Scarlet thought. "Sunny Jim seen her colors?"

"She's too far out."

"Leave us at anchor. Run the jib out, upside down. Load the guns and hide 'em. Get the crew hid, with pistol and cutlass ready." She paused to look at Pryce. "The crew's awake? Sober?"

Pryce grimaced. "About half of each."

"That'll do. We've couple of hours 'til they come up on us."

"So that's it? We send a distress signal, and try to lure them in?"

Scarlet nodded. "Might not hurt to have some of the ladies out on deck, if the right dresses can be found." She looked up at the deck beams again. "We have passengers. We are disabled – you decide how. We lure 'em in, throw over boarding cables, and take every damn piece of timber and ironwork we can pry off, short of sinking her."

"It's good to have you back, Captain."

"It's good to be here still.

"But no one has a mind for the healer, who's been up all the night, time and again." Branna glared out of her hanging chair. "Pryce, are you bothering the Captain?"

"Just getting orders. Thank ye, Captain!" Pryce disappeared and Scarlet heard her shoes tapping up the ladder.

"And you." Branna rose to her feet and ran her hands over Scarlet's throat. "Are you planning to leap up and lead the attack?"

There was nothing Scarlet would have liked better, but the look in Branna's eyes held her. "What do you think?"

"I think, after yesterday, you will have some mush and water, and a bit of rum, and go back to sleep."

"Biscuit and cheese, and some of that potion to ease the pain? And no rum, in case Pryce needs me?"

"If I bring it in, can you eat it without help? I've other wounded to look to."

"Easier than mush, with one hand. Don't bother to bring it in yourself. Let Mister Cahill send someone back. And Branna," Scarlet caught the healer's eyes. "When was the last time *you* ate?"

"I had a bite last night, but I catch your meaning. As you say, Captain."

Scarlet lay in the bunk, listening to the ship wake and come to life around her. Feet on the deck, the pleasant tone of the ship's bell, the cook rattling things in the galley, Pryce and Burgess shouting orders. Yet something was not right. She listened, concentrating, until she realized that what she missed was Flynn's voice. She would not think on that, only that she had lost a very fine officer, and that she must remember that the *Donnybrook* would not be so nimble or fast a ship without him.

A knock on the bulkhead brought her back. It was the new girl, Moreau, looking very tired but more at home in her rough clothes. She carried a plate and mug, and bobbed a curtsy before entering.

Scarlet smiled and said, "Glad you come through." The girl smiled and carried the food to the bedside table, then turned to go. Scarlet, finally feeling well enough to be bored and lonely, and called her back.

She thought first of the most obvious thing, and said, "I notice you are in the habit of givin' a curtsey. That ain't proper."

Moreau looked puzzled.

"You was taught to bend your knee to those above you. There is none above you here."

"But you are the Captain."

"Captain means more work, and more skill, and havin' the trust of the crew. It don't mean I'm of higher station. We are all equals on this ship."

More confusion. It was not the first time Scarlet had seen it. In her experience, most poor folk so accepted that their own lives were worthless that they could never be decent pirates. She tried, once again, to explain.

"You was born in some little cottage, and so was I. Pryce was born in a grand house, Burgess in a city and Mister Yeboah on a plantation where they bred slaves. Our worth is not where we come from, but who we are. And since only God can know that, it's in our interest to behave as if each of us is as valuable as all the rest." She smiled. "You stick with us, you may be a captain yourself one day, or gather up a great store of gold, and marry a lord. Or you may spend your life on your knees, scrubbing decks. You choose, now."

The look on the French girl's face was not comprehension, exactly. More like wonder. But it would do. Scarlet smiled again, lay back, and began to pick at her breakfast. Moreau's footsteps disappeared down the companionway.

Waiting was what Scarlet hated most. If she had been whole, she would have been out on deck, hauling things around, arranging the disguise, climbing up the mainmast to see the approaching ship. Sitting still in a bunk was the next best thing to hell. With her arm bound up she could not do anything useful.

The third time she overheard Pryce make some arrangement that was not exactly what she herself would have chosen, Scarlet pulled the cork from the rum bottle an began to drink.

"So this is what happens if Pryce needs you." Branna stood in the doorway.

Scarlet rolled over. "I ain't drunk."

"Of course you're not."

Excited feet pounded down the corridor, and William skidded to a stop by the open door. "Mister Pryce's compliments, Branna ma'am, and would you mind getting an axe or something and coming out on deck? She wants us with enough able-bodied folk to make a good show when we take the ship.

Branna glared at him and jerked her apron off. "So now I must be looting ships, as well as patching up these ungrateful folk? Very well, I'm coming." She turned and stabbed her finger at Scarlet. "And you. Don't go wandering about."

The sounds from above-decks kept Scarlet abreast of what was happening. Pryce ordered people into hiding, commanded them to keep still. A long wait. Scarlet stared at the rum bottle. There wasn't much left.

Ah! Now Bracegirdle was hailing the other ship. Scarlet listened with a critical ear. So, the *Donnybrook* had been attacked by pirates, and had wounded aboard. A good ploy, she'd have to remember that. The other ship, the *Cabot,* was wary. Pryce finally broke in, claiming to be a fifteen year old boy, and the captain's son, pleading for help. First mate dead, captain sorely wounded, responsibilities thrown onto the shoulders of a mere child.

Finally a shouted agreement, another wait, and the feel of the two ships bumping together.

Sudden screams and war-whoops. Scarlet would have first tried to get the other ship's officers onto the *Donnybrook* and captured. But it seemed to be working. She could feel the change in the *Donny*'s motion as the pirates bound the other ship to her. Pryce's quarterdeck voice roared out, commanding "Stand down! Stand down and you won't be hurt!"

The usual stunned silence when the crew of the other ship realized that they had been taken. Then Pryce shouting again, "Put them weapons down!"

Scarlet snapped sharply to attention. This wasn't right. If a rescue party was armed, it meant they had suspected from the beginning, and might have set traps of their own. Almost without thinking, Scarlet pushed the tangle of blankets off herself and staggered to her feet.

She heard some scuffling noises, and then a strange voice from the other ship, "Drop those pistols and get the hell off my ship, or I'll blow her brains out!"

Scarlet's mouth went dry. She had to do something. Had to. But she was dead useless in her current state. Well, maybe not quite useless, if she had a pistol.

Burgess's cabin was four steps away, and Scarlet's pistol-case stood out on his desk. She ran to the case and pried it open. Thank God she always kept cartridges and shot in it.

Shaking, Scarlet pulled the case to the bunk and sat beside it. She would have to load one-handed. She held the pistol between her knees, muzzle up, dropped a pre-measured load of powder down the barrel and fumbled for a patch and roundshot.

The tension on the decks above her was almost physical. Someone, maybe Bracegirdle, was talking. Oh, how she wished Flynn was up there now!

She pulled the little ramrod from its place under the muzzle of the gun and rammed the shot home, then flipped the gun right-way up and gripped it again. Her powder bottle would be impossible to open one-handed. Instead, she tore open another paper cartridge and used its loose powder to fill the flashpan, then closed the frizzen and checked the flint.

The strange voice shouted again. "I'll do it. If you value this woman at all, get off, every damn one of you."

Scarlet dragged herself up onto the deck. A man, probably the captain of the *Cabot*, stood on his quarterdeck, one hand wrapped in Pryce's blonde hair, the other holding a gun to her head. Pryce held her own pistol, but was bent at an angle. She couldn't turn to fire on him. Her face was more angry than frightened.

Armed sailors crowded the deck of the other ship, though most of the men hardly seemed to know how to hold their weapons. But the pirates looked barely more certain of themselves, glancing back and forth, shifting uneasily. Bracegirdle, damn him, began to lower his pistol to the deck.

Scarlet crept to the railing. Everyone was staring at Pryce, her head bent at a savage angle, the gun to her temple. The ships moved against each other with the swells. Scarlet tried to be certain of her shot. The man and woman on the deck above her were so close together, she had almost as much chance of hitting Pryce as the man holding the gun to her head.

Damn it all. Her hand was shaking. The ships jostled against each other.

Pryce saw her. Their eyes locked. Pryce smiled and winked.

Scarlet stood up. Something moved in response, on the *Cabot*'s deck, but Scarlet didn't stop. She sighted down her pistol's barrel and blew the back of the captain's head off.

Pryce tore free from the dead man's hand, took a step forward, and shot a sailor who was aiming for Scarlet. The man fell to his knees, clutching his shattered chest.

Scarlet sat down hard on the deck.

The pirates held the *Cabot* until dusk, forcing her own crew to strip her of every object of possible use. McNamara even pried loose all the glass from the captain's cabin window. When they were nearly finished, Burgess came down to report to Scarlet.

"Eighteen barrels of fine brandy, two chests of silver, one of gold. Rice, fresh biscuit, fourteen casks of dried fruit. Mister McNamara is bringing you a new desk and chair. And Bracegirdle fancied a pair of brass swivel-mounted guns they had on her quarterdeck. Thinks we can use 'em. Took all her powder and shot. Took every one of them bloody pistols."

Scarlet smiled. "Sounds like you'll be prying nails out of her woodwork, next."

"We would if anyone could figure out how."

"Sounds like a reason for a party. The crew up for it?"

"Yes, ma'am. I believe they are." Pryce stuck her head in the cabin and clasped Scarlet's hand. "Thank you."

"No matter. We were even, ten seconds later. Can you get us out of here to someplace safe?"

"Where's safe? We can head out to open water, put down a sea anchor."

"Fine. We still have a new crewmember who ain't been read in yet. And I want to put you up again. They don't have to thwart me to save me, this time."

At full dark the crew assembled on deck. Scarlet sat on deck in her new chair, behind her new desk, surrounded by a great show of their recent plunder. Folk were already digging into the fresh food Cahill had laid out.

Scarlet stood, and the talk dwindled off. "We've had a busy couple 'o days, ain't we?"

Murmurs of agreement.

"But we come through 'em. We're still here, sure, and beholden of no man. We're wiser and stronger for it. I know I am. So... Shantyman, come here will you?"

He pushed his way to the fore. "Here."

"In keeping with your captain's new-found wisdom, would you mind getting a few lads together and tipping one of them full barrels of brandy over the side? It seems I was remiss in turning over some other goods as was owed to the sea gods, and want them to know I'll be wiser the next time."

The Shantyman bowed his assent right smartly and stove in the head of the barrel with a handy axe. Everyone cheered when the amber liquid was poured over the side, for they still had plenty for themselves. Scarlet smiled and sat down.

"Second business. We have a new crewmember who needs to be read in. Mister Moreau, to the fore."

By now the girl seemed quite at home in her new clothes. Scarlet looked at her sharply. "You had a rough time here at first. It ain't this bad often, but it's a rough life, and no denying. You still willing?" The girl nodded. "You know how to make a mark? You need to sign this, after it's read."

Moreau shook her head. "Sorry, Madame Captain, I have never held a pen."

Pryce stepped over and whispered, "It's all right. I'll help you, but you must make the mark yourself." Moreau's cheeks went pink and she nodded.

"Very well," Scarlet beckoned to her quartermaster. "Mister Burgess, will you read the articles?"

Mister Burgess came forward, adjusted his glasses, and held the piece of paper up to a nearby lantern. When he began to read, the ship went dead quiet, every man and woman listening, many with their eyes closed.

"The purpose of the Donnybrook is to be a ship of freedom. To That end, all the ship's company shall have consideration for their fellows, and shall behave in accordance with that consideration. All fighting shall take place on shore. Disagreements found to be of annoyance to the Company in general shall be voted a resolution from the Company. Also- those not concerned with a matter shall not engage in a matter. Those trying to do otherwise to be voted ship's punishment.

"All matters of concern to the ship in general shall be voted on by the Company as a whole, with the following exceptions: In chase or battle, the Captain's word shall be law.

"Each member shall have weapons ready and in good order at all times. Any as do not shall be voted ships punishments.

"All the ship's company shall have full use of food, water and grog, except that rations may be voted in time of distress.

"All the ship's company shall have the right of leaving the ship upon one month's notice.

"Slavery is not recognized aboard this ship. Any slave making the deck of the ship shall be considered free. Members of the ship shall not engage in the buying or selling of persons. Violators shall be voted ship's punishment.

"Spoils to be divided in sight of all. Distributions of any spoils shall be as follows: Each full sailor shall be allotted one share. Apprentice sailors shall be allotted one half-share. Ship's officers to be allotted one and one-half share. Captain to be allotted two share. Any crew shall draw upon his share as needed, respecting Quartermaster's right of sleep and grog.

"No gambling of dice or cards shall take place in the ship. Likewise, no member of the company shall sell themselves for profit. Likewise, no member of the ship shall force another.

"No member of the company shall rob or cheat another. Violators to be stripped of possessions and put ashore at next port.

"Those wounded aboard the ship or in combat to be recompensed as follows: For the loss of a hand, foot or eye, one hundred guineas. For the loss of arm or leg, two hundred guineas. For loss of life, five hundred guineas to be sent to next of kin, if such can be found."

"These articles witnessed and signed by all, open for amendment upon the vote of the Company."

Moreau stepped forward, and with Pryce's help, made a ragged cross on the bottom of the page. Scarlet shook her hand, and let the crew cheer themselves hoarse.

"And now, all you lubbers." She rose again, and pointed an accusing finger at various members of the crew. "You thwarted me once, but I'm back against you. Mister Pryce is the finest navigator in this whole sea, keeps a cool head, and saved her captain's life today. It ain't fitting that such a woman should not be promoted. I'm putting her up for second in command, damn you, and I'll keep doing it until I'm voted a company nuisance and flogged for it. Do you hear me?"

She faced some shameful looks. Voices called out "Aye."

"And don't think to be sparing Mister Burgess's feeling. Right, Mister Burgess?"

"I am ready to retire my position, ma'am. Grateful to do it."

"I'm taking the vote myself. First vote, Burgess."

"Aye."

She pointed at each of her crew, and took the vote. Sunny Jim was contrary as usual, but the rest gave Scarlet her way.

When it was over, Burgess looked relived, and Pryce blushed with satisfaction. Celeste Moreau, standing beside her, squealed in pleasure, put her palm against Pryce's face, and kissed her full on the lips.

Scarlet started to laugh and say, "Damned French," but something stayed her. She watched as the kiss went on for too long, and then as Pryce put an arm around the French girl and leaned into it.

"Damn," said Burgess.

"Saints." Branna stood, hands on her hips, staring.

Sanchez rushed off below deck.

After another long second, Scarlet shut her gaping mouth and looked around. The Shantyman sidled up to her and whispered. "There's not a thing in the articles against it, ma'am. But it's still a matter for cryin', sure. Every fellow on this boat will find it an awful waste."

The Derelict

It was a big, old-fashioned ship, slab-sided and stubby in the masts, her sails badly worn, but still holding firm against a damp wind that threatened a storm. Overhead the sky was grey, a persistent overcast that blocked any sight of the sun.

Easy for a ship to lose its position on such a day.

The crew of the *Donnybrook* were raiders, rovers, filibusters, pirates. They had planned to raid this ship as soon as Sunny Jim had seen it rise up over the horizon. On this strange shadowless day, time seemed to stand still. The *Donnybrook*'s sail was taut. When Dark Maire cast the log-line, it showed they were making eight knots.

The ship before them fled before the wind, south-so 'west, at perhaps three. Closing speed of five knots. Unless the prey sighted them and fled. Less, if the merchant ship was fooled, and answered a friendly signal.

The *Donnybrook*'s black flag was bent to the mast, waiting to break out when the time was ripe. But the time was not ripe. The merchant ship grew slowly, steadily nearer as the dark-blue water slipped under the *Donny*'s bow.

Scarlet paced the deck, her wounded arm bound to her side, a jittery wash of nerves keeping her moving, though exhaustion already dragged at her. Her crew needed plunder, needed action, needed to become predators again after being prey to half-mad natives. She fidgeted and watched the ancient ship grow slowly nearer.

Not quickly enough. Not nearly quick enough.

Branna came up from below with a steaming mug of something the dark-green color of rotting fruit. She held it out, and when Scarlet sniffed and turned away, put a fist to her ample hip and scowled.

"You'll drink this, or I'll call a vote and take your captaincy from you and put you in bed to rest."

Scarlet's eyes strayed again to the silent ship they followed. "You can't do that, we're in chase."

"I won't need to if you're after collapsing on this very deck." Branna held out the mug again, meeting Scarlet's defiant eyes. "You know, you could still lose that arm."

At that Scarlet took the mug and gagged down the foul liquid it contained. It made her head swim and her knees suddenly week, and she glared at the healer. "You mean to put me off my feet."

"Of course I do." Branna produced another mug from somewhere, this time of beer, and handed it over. "Oh, don't worry. I have a place set together for you to sleep on deck, and the Shantyman," she glanced up with a smile at that individual, who had been loitering about conveniently, "will sing you a lullaby. That ship is three hours away at best."

Scarlet drank the beer, eager to get the foul taste of Branna's potion out of her mouth, and realized too late that the mix of hops and alcohol and whatever the vile green liquid had been would indeed drug her to sleep. She fairly swayed, and Branna led her to a large coil of rope that had been graced with a cushion. Scarlet collapsed into it, and the last thing she remembered was the Shantyman's voice, murmuring over her some strange pagan tune.

She woke late, the red rays of the westering sun shining up under the still-heavy cover of clouds, giving a peculiar glow to objects and making the very air shimmer. Scarlet crossed herself. "Elf light," she muttered. When the sun's rays at twilight came like this, unnaturally bright yet casting no shadows, the Fair Folk might wander into the Land of Mortals, stealing children and souls without discrimination.

She clambered to her feet, difficult with her arm bound and her knees still unsteady, and looked toward the quarry. Less than a mile away. She called out at random, "Does she answer a hail?"

"She does not," answered Darby.

Scarlet noticed then how unnaturally quiet her crew had grown. No one laughed or joked or spun tales of what they would do with captured gold. No one was dressed for battle, though pistols and swords were in evidence. Instead, the men and women of the *Donnybrook*'s crew went about their tasks in silence, pausing only to glance uneasily at the strange ship.

Close, she was strange indeed. The style of her hull had gone out of fashion fifty years before, and her wood was weathered and unpainted. Some of the fancywork around her high stern had so fallen into decay that it was dropping to bits.

Scarlet looked up to the masthead and decided not to risk a climb. Instead she sent Pryce aloft. "Don't let them bastards panic over some odd behavior," Scarlet said softly as Pryce put her hands on the ropes. "Just tell us what's going on."

Pryce nodded, climbed, and stood looking at the strange ship, one hand shading her eyes from the bloody rays of the sun. Then, quick as thought, she slid down the backstay to stand by Scarlet's side.

"You may not wish to hear this," she said, low. "But there's bodies lying on the deck over there, and I don't think they're asleep. You know damn well Sunny Jim will cry plague, and I don't see a thing to prove him wrong."

Scarlet chewed on her lower lip. "How do they look? Was they killed? Or died natural?"

Pryce rubbed at her cheek. "They ain't... ain't fresh. And there was blood on the deck, I think. Dark stains."

"Well, then we come in and see. " Scarlet ran up to the quarter deck and whistled to get the attention of her crew. When they turned to look, she called out, cheerful as possible.

"Well, we have got what we did not expect. There's dead men on that ship. Looks like a fight. Chances are they already been raided, but there's no way to tell for sure, and raiders may have left some treasure or goods behind." She looked into the eyes of her crew and decided they still seemed too nervous. "Besides," she went on, "I'm a might curious about why a ship would still be sailing if she's been took and stripped. I mean to go over and have a look. Any as wishes can come along."

That was it, she thought. The right tone had been struck, a mix of business-as-usual and curiosity. Curiosity would get them every time.

Pryce hailed the ship twice more as they came up. Still no reply.

Several folk headed below when they finally bumped alongside the old vessel, and several more stood with vinegar-soaked rags held to their faces. Scarlet smelled the tang of the vinegar and wished she had thought of it herself. But she needed to appear confident. She stood on the rail and called out, "Who's with me?"

Branna, of all folk, stopped passing out vinegar and said, "I'll come!" Scarlet was grateful to her.

Pryce stood mute.

Darby scratched the back of one leg with his foot, and looked at the deck.

William raised his thin, high voice. "I'll go!" Scarlet wished she could hold him back, keep him safe. But it was his lookout, same as anyone's. And she did not dare do anything that might frighten the crew.

Finally one more voice rose. It was the Shantyman's calm baritone. "I'll come. There may be a need to lay a ghost or two." Scarlet cursed him under her breath, but he seemed perfectly composed. Perhaps the crew wouldn't panic and bolt after all.

Once the ships were bound together, Scarlet climbed up the side of the larger vessel and stood for a moment, looking over the deck.

A body lay face down, just forward of the main hatch, a dark stain soaked into the wood around it.

She had seen bodies. Plenty of them. This one was wearing a coat and stockings and buckled shoes. It was thin, sunken. Perhaps the crew had not been killed, but had become lost and died of hunger or thirst. She saw no marks of disease on the bony, exposed hand. Crossing herself, she moved forward to have a look at the fellow.

When she tried to lift his head, a chunk of scalp came away in her hand. The head fell back, limp, and rolled a little. The intact hands of the corpse had been a lie. It was not a slender man, his body still fresh. It was a creature long-dead. The hands had been turned to leather by the sun. The face was a horror.

Scarlet swallowed and crossed herself again. Aloud she said, "Sickness don't hang around nothing that old." She moved to wipe her hand on her breeches, realized that a lock of the dead man's hair still clung to her, and flung it into the sea.

With the scrap of hair gone Scarlet could see the rusted handle of a marlin spike protruding from the man's temple. The crew behind her went quiet, and Scarlet whistled. "Well. Don't look so much like sickness, does it?"

William called from the starboard side, behind the mainmast. "Hey! Here's another!"

This man had been chopped to pieces, and the boarding axe that had done it was stuck in the deck beside him, the dull metal of the head gleaming red with the sunset.

This one was violent enough that they went quiet again.

"There ain't no treasure up here," Scarlet said roughly. "Let's check the captain's cabin."

Old ships, with their tall sterns, left room enough for wonderfully high-ceilinged quarters for the ship's captain. The fading light left the space gloomy, but Scarlet found an oil lamp, struck a spark and lit it, showing a cabin that looked much like her own.

That brought her up short for a moment. She stepped in and began to explore.

The room's furniture was a mismatched collection of tables and chairs in several styles and various degrees of wear. Heavy dark-blue velvet curtains, torn and damaged by rain, had been pushed away from the open stern window. Faded papers lay about the room in disarray, a silver water ewer lay on the deck, rolling drunkenly back and forth with the motion of the ship. Various other curious articles littered the space. Smashed china statues. A carved powder horn. A woman's silk dress, nearly in rags. Beside it, a string of pearls that Scarlet put in her pocket. Several pipes also lay about, and several more liquor bottles, some empty, some not.

Scarlet stood looking about her. The wind moaned. Some of the liquor bottles had never been opened, but she had no desire to pick any of them up.

She left the cabin, carrying the lantern, an uneasy feeling prickling the back of her neck. "Let's go below."

Two more dead men lay at the foot of the companionway, their decayed, bony hands still wrapped around each other's throats. Rats skittered in the darkness, and Scarlet pushed away an image of what they must have been feeding on. Some other lump, probably another corpse, lay at the end of the passageway. The air hung thick with the smell of rot.

"Wrap these poor bastards in some canvas and heave them over the side." When Branna hesitated, Scarlet glared. "Get to it. You too, Shantyman. And I want to hear nothing of how sore your old back is… You volunteered to come over."

"I'll do it!" said William, and Scarlet sighed. "Now, don't that just shame you?" she asked the others. Then she called up to the boy. "You will not. It's heavy work, and you ain't grown yet. But you may scoot over, back to the *Donny* and tell them folk to come over and help. These ain't nothing but dead folk, cut and stabbed. No sign of sickness."

William looked unhappy, but he nodded and his face disappeared from the open hatchway.

Branna opened a cabin door, pulled a blanket from the bunk, and covered the bodies. The flame of the lantern flickered with the disturbed air, and Scarlet's nerves prickled. The space around her was not more cramped than that of her own ship, but a stomach-churning feeling was beginning to grow on her that they were being watched.

"Clean up this mess," she repeated. "And, Shantyman, keep an eye out for... Well, keep an eye out."

"That I will do, Madam."

Scarlet needed to move. She headed back towards the stern of the ship, where officer's quarters would be located.

A wide galley with glassed windows covered the stern, some sort of mess hall or social room. Broken panes let in a steady breeze, which ruffled the ragged curtains. Curious carvings covered the bulkheads, and the table and chairs were mismatched. A pistol lay out on the table top. The style of the thing was recent, but it had gone rusty and was useless. Beside it, wadded up, was a piece of dark cloth. Scarlet saw gold glinting in its folds and pulled it apart.

A dozen golden guineas spilled forth, but Scarlet's eyes were locked onto the material. The black fabric had brass grommets sewn along one side. It was a flag. And a crudely-drawn death's head, ornamented with a pair of crossed thigh-bones, marked its center.

Pirates.

"They was like us," said Scarlet, to no one in particular. "They was on the account. Could it... Could it be navy that took 'em?"

No answer. She was alone. But even she herself did not believe it. The navy ran to hangings, not murdered men left to rot on a deck.

Behind her a horrible shriek rent the air.

Scarlet turned, pulling a pistol with her good hand. Heavy steps thudded against the deck. Scarlet's heart came up in her throat, but she had only one pistol and did not want to waste her shot.

The sliding door banged open, and a pale form filled the doorway. Scarlet took a split-second to steady her hand, and recognized Pryce, ghostly in a white shirt and pale sailcloth breeches.

Very carefully, Scarlet took her finger off the trigger and turned the gun away. She unstuck her tongue from the roof of her mouth. "What was that?"

"Cat," Pryce replied. "It come out of nowhere and I stepped on it."

Scarlet laughed weakly and gestured to the table. "Get the gold."

Pryce stepped over and reached out her hand, then stood looking at the death's head.

"They was," Scarlet said, answering the unasked question. "Gents of fortune, pirates. Like us. You ever heard of a ship like this one?"

"You're the expert." Pryce swept the coins into her pocket. "This tub raises my hackles. Can we go?"

Scarlet out the pistol back in her sash and scratched at her chin. "They was fighting over something…"

A wet thudding sound came from the deck above, then another, then a splash. Pryce shuddered, and a cold finger ran down Scarlet's spine. She forced a smile. "There's one batch over the side."

Pryce said again, "Raises my hackles."

The Shantyman appeared, his face grey and streaked with sweat. "You orders have been carried out, Madam Captain. But something ain't pleased with us."

"I can tell that." Scarlet took a deep breath. "They was pirates. Pirates, and something made 'em turn on each other. I'm guessing it's loot. Spread out and find it."

The Shantyman's face went blank, and he nodded stiffly. "As you say."

"Pryce, look through the officers' cabins. Shantyman, the crew deck. Where's Branna?"

"Saying a rosary over the departed."

Scarlet sighed and pulled on the string of the St. Brigid's medal that hung around her neck. "Let her be, then. I'll go below and check the hold."

She found another lamp, checked the oil level and lit it, then headed for the companionway.

On such a tall ship, the headroom in the hold allowed someone as slight as Scarlet to walk upright. She recognized the usual: beef casks, bales of cloth, odd bits of furniture. Rice sacks had burst open and spilled their contents across the deck, and the smell of moldy biscuit was thick in her nose. All around her, rats skittered in the darkness. "Bloody cat might live for years eating this lot," she muttered as she went on.

She found it near the back hatchway, standing apart from the little pool of reddish light, gleaming in the darkness. Gold. A solid, heavy disc of gold, nearly the size of a cart wheel, worked with strange symbols. At the center of it was the image of a pagan god, a squat, thick figure, its tongue extended. It stood on a human body, the lines of the carving etched deeply into the heavy metal.

The body under the god's feet reached up with one almost skeletal hand, as if pleading. But there was no mercy. Scarlet could not tell how she knew, but she did not feel that this was a deity to ask favors from. It was a god to be appeased.

Something fell in the darkness behind her, and she jumped. She could feel the saint's metal, warm against her skin, and she found herself whispering, "Saint Brigid. You bring light into the darkness, you bring light into the darkness…"

The lantern went out.

Scarlet shrieked.

There was light, barely enough light, trickling down through the open hatch. The last of the dying day. All around her, Scarlet felt an angry presence. The ship under her feet groaned.

The pirates came down in a run, carrying lights of various sorts, Branna an oil lamp, the Shantyman a candle lantern, Pryce a sputtering tallow dip. In the growing brightness, Scarlet could see more dark blood on the deck, splashed about on surrounding barrels and chests.

The pagan god glared at her, and she glared back. When William came down last, she pointed with her good hand to the great disc of gold. "There it is. There's the bloody thing what started it. Too big to be any one bastard's share, so they fought. Well, we ain't going to fight. Shantyman, Pryce, William. Get boarding axes and cut that thing to pieces."

Underneath them, the deck shifted and the ship groaned.

"Do it!" Scarlet snapped. "We'll break this thing's power, and have treasure enough for the storm season ahead."

She felt weak in her knees, suddenly, and climbed back to the blood-spattered deck to get some air. Branna stood near the railing, calling over to the *Donny* about equipment to break up the great gold disc. Rain was beginning to fall.

The news of gold, several hundredweight of it at least, cheered the crew remarkably, and they began to go to work with a will, rigging the cargo crane with a canvas sling, bringing out axes and blacksmith's tools to break up the pagan symbol, and buckets to carry it around in.

The wind was picking up steadily, as the last of the light faded from the sky. Scarlet urged her crew forward. "Hurry. Hurry. We want to get free of this cursed ship as soon as we can."

The deck of the *Donnybrook* was crowded with lanterns and moving people. Many were making ready to come over, enthusiasm for gold casting out fear.

With no warning, an enormous explosion split the air, and the deck under Scarlet's feet pitched so hard she fell to her knees. The air and the sea and the derelict ship were lit with a brilliant white ball of hot light. Someone screamed.

Then the light turned orange-red. The mainmast was burning

The ship had been struck by lightning.

For one long moment Scarlet hoped the pattering rain might stop the fire, but tar and pitch and ancient wood were more flammable than a matchstick. Bits of flaming wood ignited the foremast mainsail and the light grew until it was bright as day.

"Cast off! Cast off!" Scarlet bellowed, scrambling to her feet and running for the railing. "Get the *Donny* clear!"

A burning ship could not be saved. A vessel moored to a burning ship might be.

"Fend off! Fend off! Back the mainsail!" Pirates scattered in all directions, running to their stations, casting off lines, hauling up buckets of seawater to douse the decks and sails.

Yeboah's huge dark form stood by the railing, boathook in hand, pushing against the mass of the burning ship.

Scarlet saw Branna come over, skirt hiked to her knees, saw Pryce leap from the tall ship's poop deck. The

Shantyman stood, facing the fire as if fascinated, one hand raised to gesture.

"William!" shouted Scarlet. "Where's William?"

The derelict's flaming mainmast burst its backstay and came crashing down forward, taking the foremast with it and turning the forward end of the ship into a solid wall of flame.

"William!"

Scarlet saw a small figure scuttling about the deck on hands and knees. The paint along the *Donnybrook's* side began to blister with the heat.

"William!"

The ships finally came apart, all the lines holding them cast off or severed. At last William stood up, holding something in his hands. "The cat!" he shouted.

"Drop the bloody thing and come over!"

William looked to right and left, seeming confused. The cat struggled in his hands. Then suddenly the Shantyman was there, taking the animal and throwing it with a powerful heave toward the *Donnybrook's* quarterdeck. The cat struck the outer edge of the railing and stuck like a fly to a wall, claws gleaming red in the firelight.

The distance between the ships was now too far to jump. Scarlet gestured to her crew. "Lower the longboat!"

Yeboah stepped up to the rail, a line in his hand, drew back his powerful arm, and cast the end of the rope toward the burning ship. William caught it, and the Shantyman bound it around their two bodies, around their waists. Then, before he had time event to signal, Yeboah jerked and they were in the water.

There was no question of swimming. Even if either of them had known how, they were being pulled along, not only by Yeboah's powerful, sweating arms, but by the *Donnybrook's* increased speed as she made way on her new course. They were under the water more than they were over it, the line that bore them throwing up a narrow white wave.

Several more hands grasped the line, and after a breathless pause, the two were hauled on deck, coughing and spluttering.

Scarlet approached William, her hand raised in a fist. "You daft fool! Over a cat! A bloody cat!"

William smiled up, past his streaming hair. "God's creature, innit?"

Scarlet stayed her hand, but just barely.

Branna brought a cloth, and the Shantyman wiped his face. The crew gathered around them as the *Donny* gathered way. The light of the burning ship turned the sea to copper.

"No luck in that haul," Pryce muttered under her breath.

"A great deal of luck," the Shantyman replied. "That we are all safe, and that there was no sign of plague, and that we had a little gold into the bargain."

He held out jagged chunk of hacked gold, the size of a hen's egg. Scarlet took it and looked it over. "Cursed gold, some would say," she mused. "But the curse lay on them what coveted it. This stuff lost them their fellowship, and damned them all."

She tossed the lump out into the moving ocean, then pulled the strand of pearls from her pocket and tossed them after it.

One by one the crew emptied their own finds into the sea. Pryce was last, pouring the guineas forth in a gleaming stream.

Scarlet watched them sink. "Mates, let this be a warning to us."

The Passage Ship

Scarlet looked through the spyglass and bit her lip. Beside her, Sunny Jim swayed from side to side, moaning a little with worry over what the next few hours would hold. At the wheel, Pryce tapped her foot with impatience. Scarlet lowered the glass and snapped it into its leather case. "Ship's meeting!" she bellowed to those below.

The crew crowded onto the deck, wounded and whole, and Scarlet trotted down the gangway. "Gather round. We need a vote on this. There's a ship in the south. A passage ship from England, it looks to be, full of fine ladies and gentlemen, and all their goods. It's twice our size, and full of crew, and Sunny Jim counts eight guns on the deck. If we take her, it'll make us for the rest of the year. If we don't, she can hurt us sore."

The *Donnybrook*'s men and women murmured among themselves. The fighting had been hard, of late, and the rewards few.

"You ever take such a ship before?" asked Dark Maire.

"I have. The *Donny* has. Two years past. It were rich enough, but the damn gentry were trouble. They forced us to kill five of 'em, for they were beyond controlling."

"Why?" asked William.

"Officers act like officers, and common sailors are cattle. Lords and ladies are used to getting their way with things, and they act like anything at all."

Dark Maire frowned and looked out over the water. "I ain't never seen a grand lady."

"I have. They are a sight of trouble."

"This is a different matter entire," Burgess added. "It won't be over in a few hours. We must work this ship over for days, maybe a week, while we search every cabin and every barrel and box in the hold. These folk hide, and they mislabel. You may find a dozen golden guineas in a little box marked "pins". We'll have to look at every single thing."

"Which means we must be sober, vigilant, and under orders for all that time." Scarlet looked sternly around the circle of faces. "Sober and under orders."

Bracegirdle sighted out across the water. "How much is on it?"

Burgess frowned. "Perhaps fifteen hundred pounds, cash. Clothes, jewelry, silver plate besides."

"Let's do it."

"I'm in," said Pryce.

Approving voices rose up, and Scarlet nodded. "Load the guns. Dress fierce, arm yourselves. She can't get away, so she may fight."

Branna followed Scarlet into the aft cabin. "You're going to lead this action."

"I am. If needs come."

"You are not well yet."

Scarlet rounded on her, eyes blazing. "And the *Donnybrook* ain't sound, and half the crew hurt. We need money and it's on that boat. The crew voted. We take it."

"Will you have a care for yourself?"

"I will even drink one of your foul potions. But hurry. I need to keep an eye on things. This boat could be dangerous."

Dressed for battle in a crimson coat and her finest feathered hat, Scarlet came up to stand beside Pryce at the wheel. "Four hours at least to come up on her, and Flynn gone. Will you steer, or should I take the wheel?"

"Steering's just work, and common sense. You still know the *Donnybrook's* points of sail better than me... D'you mind me bringing her up?"

"I would not." Scarlet looked over the crew, the deck, the spread canvas. "She may fight. Bracegirdle should be happy of that. Will you stay on this deck, and take their surrender, or shall I?"

Neither of them spoke of being driven off or sunk.

Pryce's jaw muscle worked, and she said, "I'll bring her in, and go over first."

Silence stood for a moment, then Scarlet replied, "I'm captain, and I'll lead the boarding party. You keep an eye that none of 'em tries to be a hero."

They stood for a while together, looking at wind and wave, calculating angles, until they had a course to bring them across the strange ship's stern and take the weather gage from her. Scarlet called to those hauling canvas, setting the big main sail, and the *Donnybrook* settled down to run, her bow churning the dark water to white.

At first Scarlet paced, thinking of cannon fire and musket fire and the screaming wounded. But as she called her orders to adjust sail and the long sea swells slipped away under the *Donnybrook,* her nerves steadied and she began to grin as they came up, until the name *Sparta Queen* could be seen across their prey's stern.

They came in, wind full in the *Donny's* sails, the black flag snapping above her mainmast. Scarlet watched the distance between them closing, and rolled her shoulders to ease the tension in her arms. Quietly, as if in conversation, she said, "I didn't think to say it before. Thank you for getting my cabin back in order. It looks fine."

One half of Pryce's mouth rose in a smile, though she did not take her eyes off the *Queen.* "You're welcome. I'm glad you're back in it."

The *Sparta Queen's* mainsail showed several patches, but the man on her quarterdeck stood square and showed no sign of panic, watching the *Donny* through a spyglass. Crews loaded cannons on her deck. Scarlet checked her own crew. Bracegirdle had the starboard guns loaded and run out, the port guns nearly ready.

"Pryce, how's she riding?"

"Easy, Captain. Give me a little more topsail."

"Mister Darby, Mister McBride, two reefs out the topsail. Mister Yeboah, make ready to hoist the flying jib."

A little puff of white smoke bloomed in the *Queen's* rigging and a musket ball buried itself in the deck at Scarlet's feet. She shouted up to Pryce, "They've got a rifleman on their mainmast. Let's get some guns on these bastards!"

"Count of ten, I'll go hard-a-port so Bracegirdle can fire."

Scarlet could feel her heart thumping in her chest. "Heard and noted. Bracegirdle, you ready?"

"Aye!"

Scarlet called back to Pryce, "Yeboah will haul out the jib to help bring her head around." She looked ahead. "Mister Yeboah, start hauling at the broadside. You hear?"

"Aye, Captain." His deep, even, voice helped anchor Scarlet's nerves. She wanted to be at the wheel, at the rail, and hauling line, all at the same time. More musket shots spread powder-smoke into the wind, and one of the *Donny's* crew fell to the deck. In return, half a dozen pistols barked back.

Pryce started to swear. "God damn it! Hold fire!" The *Sparta Queen* was veering to port, guns ready to rake the *Donnybrook*'s bow. Pryce started to turn with her and exchange broadsides, but Scarlet called, "Hold course! Mister Bracegirdle, to port guns!"

The *Sparta Queen*'s guns went off, one after the other, forming a wall of white smoke along the water. Scarlet heard a shot whistle by. A section of the *Donny's* rail exploded into splinters. Another shot tore through the rigging and she heard the mainsail rip.

A few breathless minutes later, holding course, the *Donnybrook* crossed the *Sparta Queen*'s wake. Bracegirdle's gun crews finally let fly. Scarlet felt the deck jerk under her feet with the kick from the *Donny's* cannons.

Yeboah strained at the jib-sheet. Two others rushed to help him, and the triangular sail leaped to life. The canvas thumped as it bellied out, the mast creaked and the *Donny* bounded forward. Pryce spun the wheel and they went to starboard tack, the big boom swinging across the deck, the *Donny* cutting so close across the other ship's wake it seemed the two would touch. Then Bracegirdle let fly with a second broadside, battering the *Sparta Queen*'s stern and tearing up the rigging.

Pryce spun the wheel again, and Scarlet called instructions to the men aloft, then ran to the rail. The merchant captain was forty feet away. Scarlet looked him in the eye and screamed, "Heave over! Heave over, damn you, or we'll sink you to the bottom, we will!"

Pryce held them alongside, and Bracegirdle's crews sweated over the guns, while sailors on the *Sparta Queen* struggled with their own reloading. Scarlet shouted orders and the *Donny*'s mainsail began to shiver as they turned back onto the port tack. The gun crews rushed to the port guns and began loading. The next broadside came just as they rolled at the top of the swell, and ripped into the *Sparta Queen*'s rigging, tearing up spars, lines and canvas. With a scream, the musket man fell forty feet from the main spar to the *Queen's* deck.

Scarlet ran back to the rail and shook her fist at the figure on the quarterdeck. "Heave over! Or you're dead, you're all bloody dead!"

She could see every detail of the man's face, his white cheeks, the thin line of his mouth, his wide, unblinking eyes. Then the mouth moved, and the hand gestured. Sailors ran into the *Sparta Queen*'s rigging and shook the wind from her sails. She lost headway and fell off, and the *Donnybrook* turned back to take her.

Scarlet stormed onto the quarterdeck, shouting "Pryce, damn you, we ain't a bloody ship-of-the-line! We don't stand to and trade broadsides! What was you thinking?"

Pryce stared that the deck, shaking her head. "Just... Did it. We have more guns, and Bracegirdle loads in good time." She looked up hopefully, but Scarlet turned back, shouting to the *Sparta Queen.* "We're coming over. The first one as causes trouble is the first one dead."

The *Donnybrook* smaller and lower to the water, clung close to the *Sparta Queen* like a wolf at the side of a wounded cow. Scarlet caught the cleats nailed to the *Queen*'s hull, scrambled up the wet rungs, and clambered through a battered hole in the *Queen's* railing. As soon as she was standing on the taller ship's deck she cocked her pistol and pushed it into the captain's face. "You fired on me. Damn you to hell."

The man's flushed, livid face looked more angry than frightened, and as his eyes ran over her and he fully grasped that she was a woman, a certain contempt showed in the twist of his mouth. Scarlet reversed her pistol and clubbed him down to his knees.

Members of the *Donnybrook's* crew were swarming over on ladders and ropes. "Put this bastard in irons and throw him in the brig," Scarlet called to those on the weather-deck, "and find me the second in command!"

Darby and the Shantyman came up and dragged the captain off. When they saw him taken away, the *Queen's* sailors, lost any scrap of fight that was left in them. They stood, shoulders drooping, and permitted Scarlet's crew to begin herding them up to the forecastle. Scarlet leaned on the rail, suddenly aware of being tired.

Over on the *Donnybrook* Branna directed wounded pirates down toward sickbay, but on the *Queen* the body of the fallen rifleman lay alone, the gun five feet from his lifeless hand.

Pryce and Burgess went down the hatch, pistols drawn, forcing a member of the *Queen's* crew down ahead of them. Scarlet straightened as Mister Yeboah came up the gantry, dragging a slender young man by the collar of his shirt. "Says he's the one," Yeboah said, dropping him to the deck.

The man fell to his knees. Scarlet liked the look of that, but she need to see his eyes as she spoke to him, so she kicked him until he crawled to his feet. Then she pressed her pistol under his chin. "What's your name?"

The Adam's apple worked in his throat. "Lawson. John Lawson."

"Your captain's in my brig, Mister Lawson, and he and a lot of other folk could be dead in a minute if you don't do as I say. You're second in command?"

Nod.

"Who's that lying on the deck in his own blood, and where'd he get that musket?"

"Lord Ashford sir... ma'am... sir. He... he had a hunting rifle, and said he would pick off your men and frighten you away."

"Well, you see what come of it. Anyone else like him among the passengers?"

"I..." The young man trailed off, his eyes watery with fear.

"Any more with guns?"

"I don't know."

"The passengers in their cabins?"

He nodded, stammered, and finally managed, "Yes."

"Well, since you don't know if any of 'em are able to shoot, you will be the one to get them out on deck. All of 'em. I want every man, woman and child on the weather deck in ten minutes. Any as is found hiding, after, will be shot on sight. Am I clear?"

"Y-yes."

"Get to it."

Lawson staggered toward the gantry. Scarlet called down to the weatherdeck, telling Dark Maire and McNamara to follow him below. Lawson saw Maire's scars and quailed, bringing a scowl and a nudge in the ribs from the one-eyed woman's pistol.

Scarlet kept an eye on things, and watched sharp as passengers came straggling up into the light, blinking and looking as confused as folk awakened before dawn. Ten, eleven men, she counted. Twelve women, six with children. They skirted the dead body, mothers trying to cover the children's eyes, one of the boys straining to see. One little girl, barely old enough to walk, shrieked in terror and pulled at her mother's hand.

When Lawson came up at the last, he squared his shoulders and looked up to the quarterdeck. "Madam. Lady Ashford has fainted. We could not bring her up."

Scarlet looked to Maire. "You could not carry her?"

Maire came fully out in the deck and looked up to the quarterdeck. "The girl is not yet sixteen, and heavy with child. I'll drag her up the hatchway if you say."

"Blessed Virgin," Scarlet thought. Aloud she said, "Have Yeboah haul her to the *Donny* and give her to Branna."

That out of the way, Scarlet strode to the quarterdeck rail and fired her pistol into the air.

Several of the women and one of the men screamed, and the pirates gave a ragged laugh. Scarlet dropped the pistol, pulled the next one from her pocket, and roared, "Listen up!" in her fiercest voice. All eyes snapped to her. "This here ship fought against me. It was a damn fool thing to do. Now..." she cocked the pistol and leveled it at a man's head, then a woman's belly, then, because it was the most horrible thing she could think to do, at the screaming little girl.

"You are all alive on my charity." Scarlet locked eyes with members of the crowd. "You see what happens to those who oppose me. If we kill you all we could loot this ship easy." Two people fell to their knees. "But I don't want the mess. Don't make me regret it."

She was about to go on when Pryce came pounding up the gangway, the look on her face saying something was wrong. Scarlet stepped back from the rail to take the news, and Pryce bent to her ear and said, low, "We can't put the passengers foreword as we thought to. The whole for'd end of the crew deck is full of cattle."

"Cattle?"

"A dozen of 'em at least. Scared and milling about in a pen."

"Shite." Scarlet's mind flew. Where else could they keep the passengers secured and out of the way? She finally nodded to Pryce and stepped back to the rail. "I'm giving you all a chance. Get back to your cabins, pull out all your valuables and leave 'em in the companionway. I want every bloody thing. Give us enough, and we won't come in looking. You'll not like it if we do. Now, get!" She let the gun go off, this time into the deck, and with only the slightest push from the pirates, the passengers bolted for below decks, weeping and praying.

"Now what's all this?" Scarlet rounded on Pryce. "Cattle? Alive? After six weeks at sea?"

"All I know it that they're taking up space."

Scarlet tried to think of any other secure spot on the ship, but just then her carpenter, McNamara, came stamping up onto the quarterdeck, fists clenched. "I've just been looking at this boat's stern. That bastard Bracegirdle hit her right at the waterline and near to sunk her. I need four men on the pumps, right now, and more to help me shore her up."

"Damn it. Find their carpenter and make him help you. Take what hands you need out of the *Queen's* crew. Get me that bastard Lawson back here. Someone get that damned body out of the way. Where's Burgess?"

Pryce answered. "Already has the manifests and taking apart chests in the hold."

Scarlet sighed. "At least something's going right. Round up what sailors McNamara don't need and send 'em to Burgess. Keep 'em under close guard, but make 'em work. Let's get what we need before the bloody ship sinks out from under us."

Yeboah came up through the hatch, carrying a pale faced woman carefully in his arms. When Yeboah leaped down to the *Donny's* deck, the girl began to thrash about and scream. He held her tight, as one might a struggling child, and took her below.

Lawson came back to the quarterdeck with Darby's pistol in the small of his back. He still shook visibly, but seemed to be trying to ignore Darby. His back was straight, at least.

Scarlet studied him, trying to decide if he was working himself up to be trouble. "Is this your first passage, Mister Lawson? And did your father, by any chance, purchase your position on this ship through money or influence?"

"It is my first voyage."

"Under this captain… What's his name again?" She hadn't had time to look at the log.

"Sheffield. Captain James Sheffield."

"That's a good job, Johnny. Do you managed to know aught about the cattle on this ship?"

"Lady Windham's dairy herd."

"A dairy herd? And where are you transporting it?"

"Spanish Towne, Jamaica."

"Lady Wyndham is traveling alone?"

"With her maid."

"Mister Lawson, you are proving useful. Continue to be so, and you will stay healthy." Scarlet thought. She needed to keep the man handy, but separated from the crew. "Darby, take this man below and make him acquainted with the pumps."

Darby grinned and prodded Lawson off the quarterdeck.

Scarlet headed down to the captain's cabin and surveyed the mess. Bracegirdle had put three shots through the aft cabin window, and two into the transom below. The captain's desk lay on its side, the bunk was smashed, shot stood embedded in the bulkhead and scattered splinters of glass and wood made her glad she was wearing boots.

As she surveyed the mess, a regular creak and rattle began below, telling her the pumps were working. Now she needed work space. She picked up a battered chair, beat out what was left of the aft window, and began pitching broken furnishings into the sea.

She was trying to get the desk back on its feet when Pryce came in. "What're you doing? Branna will have your hide."

"Just need to tip it..." Scarlet had the edge of the desk on her shoulder and was lifting with her legs. Pryce ran forward and grabbed the other side, and the desk fell upright with a heavy thud, then teetered on its three remaining legs.

"There." Scarlet held up her right arm. "See? All's well."

"I hope the rest of this goes as fine. One of the cows is down with a broken leg. I told the cook to slaughter it. If we can find the milkmaid, we can have beef, cream and butter at dinner."

A tap sounded at the door and Dark Maire entered.

Scarlet looked up from searching the desk. "You've seen your grand ladies."

"Aye, Cap'n. You are right about 'em. But we got trouble. Mister Bracegirdle has blown her full of holes, and some of the passenger cabins ain't secure. I can hear the water running in below."

Scarlet sat down on the captain's bunk. "Have you been down?" Maire shook her head. Scarlet rubbed her tongue over her teeth and thought. "Will you ask Bracegirdle and McNamara if they'd kindly step in?"

Scarlet and Pryce went on rummaging through the captain's few possession. Bracegirdle came in almost at once. Scarlet didn't speak until McNamara came tromping in after.

His shock of orange hair sticking up like windswept grass, and he was wet to the thighs and missing his coat and vest. Seeing Bracegirdle, his brows drew together like storm clouds and he raised a fist.

"None of that!" Scarlet stood up and darted between the two men. "This boat's a bloody mess. Shot holes all through her" Bracegirdle opened his mouth to reply and she cut him off. "I don't care. You are both under orders, the crew voted it for as long as we're beside this bloody ship. If you don't obey me, you can go into the brig. We pull together or the whole thing goes south. Do you comprehend me?"

McNamara raised a finger that shook with rage. "The aft end of this boat…"

Bracegirdle glared. "You know how bloody dangerous they are when they fight. I ended it, didn't I? If you can find a gunnery master on any ship in these islands who's better'n me…"

"I don't care! We need this ship to keep floating until she's looted. Can you do it, McNamara?"

McNamara gestured to his clothing. "There's three and a half feet of water in the lower hold. I need this ship's carpenter, and any carpenter's mates we can find."

Scarlet looked back and forth between her carpenter and her gunner. "Mister McNamara. Would it please you to have Bracegirdle's assistance?"

She waited. The two men glared at each other. Finally, his voice shaking. McNamara answered. "That man is a destroyer. He couldn't repair a boat if his life depended on it."

Bracegirdle opened and closed his mouth several times, then reached into his belt and drew a knife.

He held it up and started to reply and Scarlet cut him off quick. "You all voted to be under orders. So that's where you are. By the Blessed Virgin. McNamara, take what folk you need from them as is helping Burgess. Bracegirdle, get our people to help you move powder and shot to the *Donny.*"

McNamara stepped in, ignoring the knife and looked into Bracegirdle's eyes. "If you get in my way…"

Scarlet caught the gunner's arm and pulled him away. "Don't interfere with each other. If you do, if either of you do, there will be a whipping, so help me." She stared into Bracegirdle's eyes, willing him to obey her.

Pryce glared at McNamara. "D'you hear your captain? Do you? Then say 'Aye, sir!'"

McNamara muttered again and finally said, "Aye."

Scarlet gritted her teeth. "Bracegirdle?"

"Aye."

Scarlet took a deep breath. "Bracegirdle, start by going back on the *Donny*. Get the powder room opened and some ramps set up to roll barrels in there. This ship had cannons, she'll have powder and shot, too. We need 'em. Get moving."

Bracegirdle's eyes darted back and forth, finally he said, "Aye, sir!" and headed out.

McNamara glared after him. Scarlet went back to her seat and waiting until Bracegirdle was well away before speaking again. "Mister McNamara, will the pumps keep up?"

He ran a hand through his hair and sighed. "We'll need to pump constantly. I want another four men at least, to form a second shift."

"Who can we give you?"

McNamara paused for a moment. "The *Queen's* officers. We'll chain 'em to the pump handles. If they stop pumping, everyone hears the quiet. And if we wear 'em out, they'll have less energy to cause mischief."

Scarlet grinned. "A fine idea. Have Yeboah help you move 'em and get 'em chained up. I mean to look over the passenger cabins. We may need to put get 'em all up here."

She tucked her two spent pistols into her skirt's waistband and checked the priming on the two still in her pockets, told Pryce to stay put, and followed.

They had barely made it down the companionway steps when the noise stated. Scarlet recognized the sound of a fight before she saw the combatants, and pushed past Maire. It was William and a passenger of about the same size. She grabbed William by the scruff of his neck and hauled him off the boy he was pounding.

"William! That ain't proper."

William kicked and struggled for a moment, then got his feet under him. The passenger boy scrambled up, wiping his bloody nose. "He hit me!"

Scarlet turned to William. "What happened?"

"He's got a nice coat. I told 'im to take it off, and 'e wouldn't. So I hit him."

The passenger boy stepped forward, "Thief! You're a thief! My father's going to thrash you!"

Scarlet took the spent pistol from her waistband and handed it to William, barrel first. "How many times have I told you? Don't fight with 'em. Now, hit him once, proper, and take his coat."

William swung the pistol-butt and the other boy fell to the deck with a shocked look. Scarlet helped William to remove the coat, then held it out for him to slip into.

"There now. You have a good eye. It's a fine fit." She slapped William affectionately between the shoulder blades and retrieved her pistol. "Never fight with 'em. It reduces your dignity, and makes the next one think he might knock you down. Now let's get this young rogue back to his cabin."

She scooped up the sniveling passenger by his shirt and dragged him back toward a cabin where a woman's voice could be heard sobbing.

At the sound of her footsteps, more voices rose up. Some cried that the ship was sinking, some begged for mercy, others just yammered. Bracegirdle's shots had torn up the whole aft end of the ship.

The last cabin in the row, the one Scarlet had originally suspected was broken open, a shattered place in the bulkhead where the boy must have crawled out, and the sliding cabin door off the track, holding the parents inside. Under her feet Scarlet could hear water gurgling in and the rasp of the pump.

She kept her face away from the hole, and bellowed into it. "This your baggage I'm holding?"

A man's voce started to answer, but the woman drowned him out. "Allen! Oh, my God. Allen! Are you all right?"

Scarlet glanced at her burden. "I'll give him back, but you'd best be teaching him that the folk with guns are the ones in charge. William, be a good boy and pry the door open."

William cleared the track and Scarlet threw the passenger boy to his parents. The cabin was full of overturned boxes and furniture. The woman clutched at her son, but the father stood with his fists clenched, looking like trouble. Scarlet pointed the pistol at his waistcoat buttons. "You got your boy back this time. Don't let him out again, or it may not go so well." She backed out door and signaled for William to push it closed.

Maire stood near them in the passage now, and thumped her hand on another door. "This one says the sea's coming in."

The aft end of this deck was partitioned off in a dining saloon, and the *Donny's* canons had torn through the room, shattered the bulkhead and buried shot in the passenger cabins.

Scarlet looked over the lines of the cannon blasts. "There's no chance at all of anything but spray coming in there. But these cabins ain't safe. There's too much damage. Give us an hour to clear up the captain's cabin, and we'll squeeze 'em all in there."

"Aye, Cap'n." Dark Maire sketched a mock-salute in the air and Scarlet laughed, then headed back to the captain's cabin to warn Pryce.

"We've an hour to get through here and tack up some sailcloth over that window, for we're about to have visitors."

Pryce threw a handful of clothing to the deck and made a sour face. "This fellow don't have much worth looting. Old clothes, no books. Not even real silver on his shoe-buckles. Why should a ship's captain live so poor?"

"Who knows what any of 'em are about." Scarlet left Pryce scowling into the sea-chest and moved to the captain's desk where she began pulling out drawers and letting them fall to the floor. "Here we go." The bottom drawer held two bottles and a small, iron-bound chest. "Ship's payroll, I'll wager."

"Good." Pryce rose with a soft grunt. "But there's more."

Scarlet cocked her head.

"The passengers on this boat may have hid their money in amongst the dishes and the old family paintings, but they'll want some close at hand. The captain or the purser's supposed to keep it, locked up somewhere."

"All right. Do you want to stay here or move to the purser's room?"

"I'll move, if you don't mind. This fellow's got on my nerves."

"All right."

Scarlet handed over the chest, then bent over the desk again as Pryce staggered out, hauling the chest into the companionway.

This one was a hoarder. Scarlet felt it in her bones. There would be money hid in unlikely places. She tore all the drawers out of the desk and felt for hidden compartments, but found nothing. Damn.

She went to the bunk next, throwing blankets and pillows onto the floor, then dragging off the mattress. A little channel had been crudely carved into the headboard, below where the mattress would lay, a neat stack of silver pounds lay stacked along it. That was one. She slipped the casing off a pillow and stuffed it with coins.

She had said to bring the passengers up in an hour, and felt the time ticking. The two boats were drifting, bound together, and anyone sighting them would see at once that something was amiss. She didn't want to spend days crawling over the captured ship. She wanted the *Queen's* money, and her most valuable cargo, and she wanted to leave, quick. Only with all the lines cut and the *Donnybrook's* mainsail out full would they be safe again.

One of the drawers under the bunk had a false bottom.

Once again the hidden coins were silver. Scarlet swore to herself, even as she shook the coins into her bag. This captain had been hoarding all right. This money looked like embezzlement. A shilling here and a pound there, stinting the crew on pay, cutting corners on supplies. But somewhere there was real money, gold, captain's wages, likely years of it.

The mattress was too light to be holding valuables. She had searched the desk. Pryce had been pretty through with the sea-chest... Her eyes wandered over the bulkheads.

Ah! There. A little cabinet, built into the wall, almost hidden behind a hat and a cheap dress-sword hung on a peg. Scarlet examined the dress-sword. It was all show, nearly useless as a weapon and not valuable enough to keep. She tossed it out the broken window.

The cabinet held silver-plate, rather a lot of it, a huge platter, serving dishes, candlesticks. That was better. A captain had to entertain, after all. Scarlet made a pile and carried it out, then examined the interior of the cabinet minutely. The space was dark and irregularly shaped, but didn't seem to hold any secrets.

Well, maybe she could reckon a way to persuade the captain to tell her where his fortune was hid. In the meantime, she needed the back window covered over, and some provisions to lock the door. She picked up the bag of coins, then went back for the ship's log. It had been a busy day so far, but she must make some time to read up on what the *Sparta Queen's* officers and men had been up to.

"Mister F…" Scarlet caught herself. She had been about to say, "Flynn," and Flynn was food for the fishes now. Instead she called, "Darby! Sanchez! Front and center, I need you!"

Her crewmembers had been loitering about the main hatch, and come down smart enough when they heard her call. "Here." She slung over the bag, and nudged the plate and chest with her toe. "Take all this to the *Donny* and stow it, then come back with tools and a length of sailcloth and secure this stern window. I mean to put passengers in this cabin, and I don't want any wondering off."

"Aye, Cap'n." They loaded up and headed up the ladder. Scarlet checked the opposite side of the cabin, but there seemed to be no cabinet on that side. Then she took up the logbook and stuck her nose in where Pryce was searching.

"Any luck?"

Pryce was at the purser's desk, with an account-book open before her. "Numbers, but no locations. From what I can tell, there's about two thousand pounds cash checked in for safe keeping. There's a separate fund for payroll and ship's operation."

Scarlet nodded. "That chest we found is one of those. Well, if we can find that cash, it won't much matter what else we take. No sign of it here, I suppose?"

"None." Pryce rubbed her chin thoughtfully. "Do you think Burgess could find it?"

"Burgess is busy. I'll go straight to the captain. I don't like him much. He's in our brig, and likely scared. It shouldn't take much to scare him more."

Pryce shrugged. "As you will. You done with the cabin?"

"Give it one more go-round. I found a cabinet on the starboard side, but none to port. Where's Mister Yeboah?"

"Working the cargo crane when last I saw."

Scarlet carried the logbook to her own cabin, picked up a lantern, then paused by the capstan to draft Yeboah for her task. "Now listen," she told him as the moved forward toward the *Donnybrook's* brig. "I know you don't like hurting folk, but I need you to look a right murderer for this. If the man's scared enough we won't have to hurt him, and I don't want it to get messy. Give me an angry look." She examined the man's scowl and shrugged. "Good enough. Now let's see what we can do."

The brig was on the orlop deck, below the waterline, far forward past all the cargo and supplies. The deck above was so low that Scarlet had to duck under the beams, and Yeboah was bent nearly double. In the very tip of the bow was a small, triangular cage, where the *Queen's* captain sat, blinking in the sudden light form the lantern.

"Jimmy Sheffield!" Scarlet shouted. "You rum bastard. You're guilty of embezzling company funds, and shorting your crew's pay. You fired on my ship besides. Do you want me to take flesh and blood to pay for all the folk you've wronged, or do you have something else I'd like better?"

Captain Sheffield, sitting on the brig floor, his wig askew and a great bruise rising under his left eye, did his best to look outraged. "You villain. You trollop. How dare you threaten me? When the authorities hear of this…"

Scarlet leaned in close. "There ain't no authorities. There is you, and me, and this man here, who lost a dear friend in one of your bloody broadsides and would like payback." They had taken no serious casualties, but Yeboah could be counted on to play along. "Now, you tell me what I want to know, and I might keep control of my man. Or not. It's up to you."

Behind her, Yeboah made a deep growling sound. Captain Sheffield went pale, but kept most of his composure. "I'll see you hang for this."

"If you live." Scarlet leaned in close. "I have the silver from your bunk, and the gold from your desk, and the plate, and the payroll. What I want is the passengers' funds. You've suffered enough. Let someone else pay me."

That had got him, that his precious money was already gone. She saw the sweat break out on his brow, and his throat work as he swallowed. Yeboah made another threatening noise and Scarlet got out of the way, enabling Yeboah to put one huge hand around the man's neck. Sheffield turned turkey-red and his eyes bulged before Scarlet called out a curt Belay that!" Yeboah dropped the man to the deck and backed off, and she came in close again as Sheffield coughed and sputtered. For a moment she thought they'd broken him, but then his eyes cleared and drew narrow. He had thought of something.

"If you kill me," he rasped, "You'll have nothing."

Scarlet growled under her breath and stood up as high as she could. "Very well then," she told him. "We'll heat up some irons, and see what we can do to persuade you further." She pushed past Yeboah, taking the lantern with her. She heard Yeboah say something behind her, and the rattle of iron bars. She waited at the hatch, watching a cargo net full of barrels come over, until Yeboah was beside her.

"We gonna talk to him?" the big man asked, and Scarlet shook her head. "Let's wait until tomorrow. He can stew, and I can think."

Darby was riding with the barrels, and gave a whoop as the net touched down. "Last one before supper. Cookie's boiled fresh beef!"

Up to the *Donny's* main deck, then down below on the *Queen*. Sure enough Mister Cahill, the ship's cook, was setting up food on the crew deck, boiled peas and biscuit and the beef, smelling mighty good. As she watched, Burgess herded his group up from the cargo deck. They stood milling, uncertain, and Scarlet picked up a wooden platter and thrust it into the hands of the man nearest her.

"Well, get to it. Take what you want, there's plenty."

The man approached the pots and seemed surprised when Cahill and William ladled out the food. Scarlet stepped into the line next, picking up a tin plate and a spoon from the mismatched stacks. The sailors still seemed reluctant, but she left Burgess to urge them on.

She tucked in, hungry, and was just finishing up when Cahill sat down beside her. His hair was as greasy as always, his shirt, with the arms ripped off, was no more or less stained, and his apron just as worn. But there was a certain tension about him that made Scarlet take notice. "What is it, man?"

"Cap'n! I want you to see something."

"What is it?"

"It's... It's just the most beautiful thing in the world."

Scarlet smiled. "You ain't allowed to molest the passengers, and you know it."

"It ain't nothing like that. It's a... Well, come and see."

Mystified, Scarlet got to her feet and followed as Cahill led her aft. Finally he stepped back gesturing grandly to something out of sight of the passageway. Scarlet moved forward and sighted a huge iron thing, large as a captain's bunk, glowing with heat and swaying on chains anchored in the beams above. It looked like nothing she had ever seen before.

"What in Mary's name is it?"

"A stove, Cap'n. A modern stove." He began to open and close little doors, pointing out a roasting spit, two ovens, and something called a warming pan which mystified Scarlet entirely.

"And what has all this to do with me?"

"I want it, Captain."

"This?" Scarlet stepped back and stared at the thing. "It will weigh a ton at least! It's... It's bloody built into the ship."

"I don't care." The cook dropped his delighted smile as if it was something hot, and rounded on Scarlet. "You've no idea what it's like cooking in this climate, hot as hell, the damn deck pitching and boiled beans flying all over the place. Mice in the hams and weevils in the flour. Do I ever ask for anything?"

"You ask for salt and spice and cabbages and pigs and I don't know what."

"For you all, for your damned breakfast, lunch and dinner. I never asked nothing for myself. Now, damn it, I want this stove. You can get it moved if you want to. If you don't, I'll call a vote, or get off the damn *Donnybrook*, or start a mutiny. I want this thing and I'll have it."

Scarlet held up her hands. "Peace. I'll do what I can. The thing's glowing hot, and we've two decks above us, and I don't know how big the hatch is. Throw some seawater on it and cool it down. I'll pry McNamara loose from the bilge and have him take a look."

Mister Cahill wiped his hands on his greasy apron. "I'll cool it off once I've got the rest of the cow boiled. Beef soup for dinner tomorrow."

"Now we're stealing a stove," Scarlet said, back in the captain's cabin.

Pryce looked up from where she had been digging at the planks with a knife. "A stove? No, don't tell me, I don't want to know. This is the sneakiest man I ever saw. I cannot find where that money is hid. Any luck talking to him?"

"He's holding out. Knows we can't kill him outright, and lacks imagination. Maybe expects a reward for keeping the passengers' money safe. We must persuade him some way. No one took dinner over, did they?"

"Not as I know. Are we putting passengers in here?"

"Right now. Just wanted to check out the patch job. Looks all right."

Pryce stood. "I'll take the first guard duty on the door. We should put a couple of people on the quarterdeck as well, in case they feel like trying to get away."

The tropical sun was nearly at the horizon. Scarlet stood at the quarterdeck rail and called her crew. "We'll be moving the passengers to the captain's cabin." Her eyes flew over the faces. "Mister McNamara, get me that first mate up. What's his name, Lawson? Yeboah, Oort, you two will go with him to open the cabins. Get the folk out, clear the cabins, and pass 'em down the line. Pistols out. We'll shuttle 'em into the big cabin, right down the line."

The pirates moved to form a gauntlet, and after a few moments Scarlet could hear Oort shouting, "Get along der, get out!" The results were noisy enough to carry. The men complained the women wept, and the children screamed. Scarlet waited on the quarterdeck, looking off the rail, a pistol in each hand. The first people up, blinking in the light and shaking, was the family of the adventuresome boy who had forfeited his coat. The child looked much more subdued, and one eye was swollen nearly shut.

Scarlet's crew had spread themselves along the deck, and laughed as they herded the passengers along, shoving and slapping. As one woman moved down the line, Dark Maire stepped forward and pulled a necklace from her. The passenger clutched at it, at the same time recoiling from Maire's scars. The woman's husband tried to fight Maire off, but Darby put a pistol in his face and he backed down.

All the folk complained as they saw the space they were herded into, and as the last of them were pushed in Scarlet decided to give them a few words of encouragement.

She called Darby to her, and Yeboah as the man came up, and banged the cabin doors open. The folk fell back at her appearance, muttering and weeping. She looked them over – the place was crowded, but not worse than the *Donny's* crew deck on a rainy afternoon.

"There now!" she shouted, making herself heard. "I told you folk you wouldn't like it if we had to go searching, but you ain't turned over the goods, so we must find them. You'll stay here until we're done. Anyone wants to help us find cash, you'll be given consideration."

"Damn you!" cried one of the men, and a woman hissed, "Devil."

"That's all well and good…" Scarlet paused when an old woman hobbled forward and demanded, "What about my cattle?"

"What about them?"

"You can't kill my cows. They have pedigrees."

Scarlet had no idea what a pedigree was. She answered plain and simple. "Well, I reckon we can do anything we want. We have eaten one, what was too hurt to live, and we will take 'em with us if we decide to."

"You can't do that." The only woman stamped her foot. "They are my husband's property, the foundation of our dairy herd. Are they being fed properly? Are they being watered? They're nervous animals. They need to be cared for. Are they being milked correctly?"

Scarlet laughed at that. "I reckon one or two folk know how to milk a cow. But maybe your milkmaid should have a look. Which one is she?"

The old woman tried to give no sign, but her eyes flicked to a young woman in a plain wool dress. Scarlet signaled Darby and said, "Take her." Darby grabbed the girl by her wrist and pulled her from the room.

The girl shrieked and clawed at the woodwork as she was dragged through the doorway. Women screamed and the old lady came at Scarlet with her cane raised. Scarlet's instinct was to strike back, but instead she got out of the way and backed toward the door.

Yeboah covered her retreat. She paused at the door and said, "If you calm down, there will be food and water. If you don't want it, just keep making a fuss." She slammed the door and shot home the makeshift lock.

Darby had the milkmaid by the shoulders. "What do I do with her, Cap'n?"

"Make her disappear for a while. Take her to the cattle and shut her in with 'em." She looked at the girl. "You can get out of this in one piece if you do what we say. I want those cows cared for and milked. You do that, we're happy. You gather that?"

The girl nodded and William came up and led her away, looking happy to have someone to order around. Scarlet shouted through the door. "I tell you, let on where the money is, and all this will end!"

Night was coming on fast, and as Scarlet walked the gangway back to the *Donnybrook* she felt full tired after a hard day. Yet there was still the logbook to read, and no doubt folk stopping in to ask questions or complain about this or that.

Even her feet hurt, and once she was back in her own cabin she kicked off her boots and sat at the big desk, running her fingers through her hair. Damn. She wanted nothing so much as a long drink of whiskey and eight hours in her bunk.

A tap at the door and Branna came in carrying a candle. "And what are you doing here, sitting in the dark?"

Without asking leave, she stepped forward and lit the hanging oil lamp, then the candle on Scarlet's desk.

Scarlet sighed. "You've brought me something foul to drink, I imagine?"

Branna held out a tankard, and Scarlet pinched her nose shut and poured it down her throat. When she could stand no more she came up gagging, and glared at Branna's smile. "There. Are you pleased?"

"A bit." Branna pulled up a chair and sat. "I thought you might like to know how it is with the girl you sent over."

"Girl?" Scarlet thought. "The one whose husband is dead? Well, how is she? Please don't say we have a baby coming, for every woman in the crew will want to help, and I'll lose all my best workers."

Branna took a long breath and let it out in a careful sigh. "Not yet. She had a dreadful shock, she did, and she ain't well with it."

"And I'm supposed to do what?"

"You might try to keep down all the shouting and the holy terror."

Scarlet laughed. "You know fear is our stock-in-trade. I can't help it."

"Well, do what you can. I wouldn't mind delivering a child, but this one should stay in the mother for another half month at least."

"I'll take it under consideration." Scarlet yawned mightily. "What did you give me?"

Branna smiled. "Never you mind, but sleep while you can."

Scarlet shrugged her coat onto the chair behind her and took off her belt. No use to try reading the logbook now, she'd be sleep on the desk in seconds. Instead she scrabbled in her pockets for a pistol, took out her kit from the desk drawer and began reloading.

"Captain…" The Shantyman didn't even bother to tap, just stuck his curious nose in, followed by the rest of him. "A word?"

"And where have you been all the day long? I've looked over these two ships from noon to sunset, and not an inch of your coat have I seen."

"I was aloft, madam, keeping watch against our enemies."

"More like you were hiding from any work as needed done. Well, what do you want now? A golden chamberpot or my own cabin for some assignation you've arranged?"

"I wished to point out that the ship we're looting has an uncommon fine captain's gig, and I've a feeling it may come in handy."

Scarlet's tired mind spun around until it landed on the pretty little boat stored amidships on the *Sparta Queen's* main deck. "Well, if you fancy it, pick it up and carry it over."

"I meant to ask if you could assign some folk to the task, for me old back…"

"Your old back did you quite fine when you was carrying off that woman at the port in Martinique. If you want…"

"I am one hundred and fifty-seven years old…"

"Oh, go on with you, you keep saying all that, and not one spot of proof do you offer…"

"Sailed with Drake, I did, and discovered the secret of the winds…"

"And now you won't do a lick of work…"

"Giving you my sage advice, won from the sea gods themselves…"

"Over a bloody boat, which you'll never lift an oar to row, you villain…"

The door banged open. "And a grand spot of quiet you keep us in, Captain, with your fine soft voice and the way you have of getting' on with the crew!" Branna had her hands on her hips, and looked as much like a thunderstorm as a woman. She glared from Scarlet to the Shantyman and back again. "Well? Who'll stand by me to catch this babe, for it'll be coming soon at this rate!"

Scarlet gathered herself and spoke to the Shantyman with quiet dignity. "You may bring the gig over at your convenience, and take Moreau and Sanchez to help you, if you can pry 'em loose from honest work. Will that do?"

The Shantyman nodded and gave one of his odd, antique bows. "Thank'ee, milady."

Scarlet had one last idea, and grinned as she spoke to Branna. "And if you'd dose this man with something for his aching back, for it seems he's hurt it while watching the horizon today."

"That I will." Branna grasped the Shantyman by the collar and led him out. Scarlet watched them go, looked back to the pistol on her desk, then sighed and put her head down to sleep.

She woke feeling better than she had expected. Dawn spilled pink light through her cabin window. Her lamp had burned itself out, and the candle was just about to gutter. She stood, stretched, and wandered out to the deck for a dipper of water. No one was stirring yet on the *Queen*, but Mister Cahill was singing and banging pots belowdeck.

She wanted a fresh shirt, but made do with pouring more water over herself before buckling on her belt and tucking in a pair of pistols. She didn't bother with her boots.

McNamara was asleep halfway down the ladder to the orlop deck, one arm wrapped around the rungs, a leg dangling, head hanging down. Below him the pumps clattered on, slow but steady.

Scarlet reached down and shook him.

He jumped, nearly fell, and said, "The pumps have slowed," while looking around as if he didn't know where he was.

Scarlet scooted down until she was perched beside him. "It don't sound too bad. Take me down and show me how she lies."

The bilge had come up, and the orlop deck lay under ten inches of stinking water, but a high damp mark on the bulkhead showed how bad it had been only the day before. McNamara took Scarlet aft and pointed out the oakum pounded between the loosened planks, new timber put up, and a pot of pitch put by to finish the job.

"It's a fine job you've done here," Scarlet told him. "With some fresh men, we may have her dry by noon."

McNamara shook his head. "There's something not right in her bottom. She ain't sound."

She clapped him on the shoulder. "It ain't your job to make her sound, only to keep her from sinking as long as we're here. I'll see to getting the pump crew changed. Go and sleep proper."

McNamara rubbed his eyes. "I've rested."

"No, you ain't. You've dozed a little. Sleep, and save your hero's effort for when the *Donny* needs you."

He looked at her with a bleary eye. "You want somethin' Captain?"

"I do at that, and am hoping you don't throw me into the ocean when I ask. Now, get some rest." He gave a scoffing laugh, but headed up the ladder, while Scarlet went to gather help for the pump crew.

Sanchez and Darby helped her select four stout male passengers from the captain's cabin and drag them out. The ship's officers, chained to the pump handles, were nearly dead of exhaustion. They stumbled and staggered their way to the *Queen's* brig, and offered no resistance as they were locked in.

By now folk were stirring in earnest, and Mister Cahill began to ring the bell, calling the crew to breakfast. Scarlet held her bowl and received a generous ladle of cereal. She smelled and grinned. "Oatmeal porridge! It's been a year, if it's been a day."

Cahill held up a pitcher. "Fresh cow's milk. Twenty-nine gallons this morning. And cream for the tea. Your dairy maid has been very busy."

"That's grand. Living like gentry, we are, now. I'll see about your stove, soon as McNamara is on his feet again."

The tea was white with heavy cream, and Scarlet smacked her lips over it, and ate a double portion of the oatmeal. It reminded her of her family's farm, where she had milked the cow herself.

A certain part of her wanted to have that again, the early morning quiet, the warm animal, and the quiet patter of milk hitting the side of the bucket. Maybe tomorrow. She took a second mug of tea back to her desk, and at last sat down to read the logbook. With a finger under the line, she began to puzzle out the words.

Navigation coordinates, those were easy, and she pulled out a chart to trace where the *Queen* had been, just a straight haul over from England, no great surprise. Harder to read were the notes of ship's day-to-day business. She knew certain words, and concentrated on them, noting two flogging over the last two weeks, one for theft, and one for something she thought was drunkenness, but could not be sure. Captain Sheffield was a stern man with his crew, but not vicious. She poured over the entries, but could see nothing useful, except a scrawled note about water that she simply could not decipher. She went over the words carefully, one letter at a time, but the writing refused to release its secrets. She sat back. Water was the most important thing on a ship. Finally she carried the book below and tapped on Pryce's cabin door.

Pryce slid the door in its track and glared. Her hair stood on end, and she wore nothing but a shirt. Behind her in the bunk, Moreau blinked and pulled the sheet up.

"I need you to read this." Scarlet said and thrust the book forward.

"Good morning to you, too." Pryce turned the book right-side up. "I ain't malingering. Some of us were keeping watch last night, you know."

"Branna drugged me. Read it and I'll go."

"You're welcome." Pryce squinted in the passageway's dim light. "Don't this fool ever sharpen his quill? Let me see… July twenty-third, is that it? 'Water short, reduced ration to one and a quarter pints, may need to short cattle next…'" She looked up sharply. "Shorting the men that bad, and not the cattle?"

"Bastard gets flogged for that." Scarlet took the book back. "I need to make sure we give the crew as much as they want to drink today. Damn me for not reading this sooner."

"Ain't your fault." Pryce glanced over her shoulder at Moreau. "*Se réveiller, cheri.* We have another busy day."

Burgess stood, in shirtsleeves and breeches, watching as the *Queen's* sailors finished breakfast. Scarlet hated to see all the good oatmeal going down those unfamiliar throats, but pirate rules were that everyone ate the same. Burgess looked tired and unshaven, and a black smudge decorated his forehead.

"Have these men drunk as much as they would like this morning?" Scarlet asked, with no preamble. The sailors glanced back and forth, shoulders suddenly hunched, frightened.

"They've had water," Burgess replied. "I can't say how much. No one's complained."

"Well they might, for they've had hardly more than half a ration for these past ten days. Send someone to open a butt of water, and let them all stand until they've drunk their fill."

For this chore there were actually volunteers, and while a cask of water was brought out and tapped, Scarlet had a few quiet words with her quartermaster.

"Pryce reckons there's at least two thousand in passenger's cash, marked down by the purser and held for safe keeping. Pryce and I tore the aft cabin apart, and she looked through the purser's office, and not a cent of it could we find. Have you any idea?"

Burgess rubbed at the bristles on his cheek and sighed. "I suppose I should go and look through the purser's office myself. Have you spoken to the man?"

"He was pumping bilge-water most of last night. You may find him locked in the aft cabin."

"Then I'll step back and have a word. Would Pryce care to come along?"

"Go and find her." Scarlet nodded to the hatch. "I'll take up here. How are you sorting it?"

"I'm taking all the barrels of chinaware, and anything like bolts of cloth. Furniture I'm putting aft, to be loaded on the *Donnybrook* last. Apart from that, it's just opening the crates and going through them.

Burgess moved off, and Scarlet began to shoo the sailors who had finished their water into the hold. A good drink had done them a world of good, and several bowed to her as they went to their work, or knuckled their foreheads in respect.

The men had picked up a routine for breaking into the passengers' possessions. Eight of them had taken to simply shifting cargo, while other methodically opened barrels and chests for the pirates to inspect. When Darby rode the cargo net down through the open hatch, two barrels of china went into it at once, and then the men took a rest while Scarlet decided which crates to take outright, and which to sort through.

The passengers owned more odds and ends than made any sense at all – paintings and tapestries, carpets, whole crates of books. One box held nothing but endless bundles of papers. Scarlet sorted through it all as best she could, and was happy to see Burgess, washed and shaved, coming down the ladder.

"He tell you anything?" she asked, stretching her back.

"I believe the man expects some great reward if he can fox us, Captain."

"I caught the same off the captain. Any thoughts?"

Burgess straightened his glasses. "Is there some charm for it?"

Scarlet sat on a box and pulled her feet up to sit cross-legged. "Finding something lost is one thing, Finding something hid, now that's another. It's either easier, or it's harder than it seems."

Burgess shook his head. "It is not my business. I shall return to counting pewter plates, with your permission."

An angry shout broke loose on the deck above and Scarlet leaped off the box and dashed up the ladder. Bracegirdle and McNamara were squared off on the *Donny's* deck, voices rising by the second. As she watched, McNamara drew back a fist and punched Bracegirdle n the jaw, rocking him back and bringing a roar of rage.

In another second the two men were rolling on the deck, shouting and kicking. Scarlet leaped down to the *Donny*, not bothering with any of the ladders, and jerked both men to their feet in a rush of pure rage.

Bracegirdle had his damned knife out again, Scarlet slapped it away, then slapped him on the cheek, hard enough to bring him back to himself. She could hear McNamara breathing behind her in ragged gasps. She took a step back so she could see them both and demanded, "What the hell's going on here?"

"Lazy bleeder..."

"Fekken gombeen..."

"Shut your gobs, the both of you! You are both under orders, damn it. I said I'd call for a flogging, and I will." She looked from one to the other, suddenly aware that she couldn't clap McNamara in irons, not with a stove that needed moving the *Queen* leaking like an old shoe on a wet day. And if she didn't chain McNamara, she couldn't very well chain Bracegirdle, knife or no.

Part of her wished that she had been knifed. It would make things clearer. Instead she was left standing in the middle of the deck with two officers who were due a whipping, and a lot of eyes on them.

She grabbed them both by the ears and dragged them in close. "Now listen, you fools, this is how it falls out. You are under orders. I have told you both to act like gentlemen, and you have not."

McNamara tried to speak, and Scarlet cut him off. "You are making a fool of your own captain in front of a lot of civilians, and I won't stand for it. You are both on report. We will have a proper trial when we are back under sail. Until then, you will work or sit in your cabins. Do I make myself clear?"

This time it was Bracegirdle's turn to open his mouth. Scarlet glared at him. Bracegirdle shut his mouth. She kept staring until he glanced down at the deck and muttered, "Aye, Cap'n."

"All right then. Bracegirdle, get below and help Mister Burgess sort cargo. Mister McNamara, follow me."

Scarlet clambered back over to the *Queen* with both men following, and saw Bracegirdle down to the cargo deck, then led McNamara to the galley.

Cahill had left the stove unfired, cool, and cleaned, and had gone so far as to set a man to pulling up all the tin deck plating meant to catch falling coals. The sailor scrambled to his feet and bobbed his head to Scarlet in nervous respect.

"Mister Cahill has requested that we rip this here stove out of the *Queen* and install it on the *Donnybrook.* I imagine our old stove will come over here. This morning, I would have asked if you could do it. Now I'm telling you. Move it."

McNamara looked the thing over, his face growing pale. "It may not go through our hatch."

"Make it go."

"It must weigh a ton and a half."

"I don't care. Mister Cahill ain't been brawling with his fellow-officers like a tavern sot. You will have it out of here, and you will install it in our own galley, and you will be prompt about it. Am I clear, Mister McNamara?"

"Aye, Cap'n."

Scarlet wanted to stamp up the ladder, but could not, as she was barefoot. She climbed with as much dignity as she could muster, came out on deck, and nearly ran into the Shantyman, who was hovering about the hatch. "What do you want?" she demanded, before he had a chance to speak.

"Would you help me to procure some help to move this gig?" He gestured extravagantly to the ship's boat, secured upside down in its place on the deck.

Scarlet had to admit it was a pretty little thing, half the size of the *Donny's* longboat, brightly painted in green and yellow, with fine lines and a delicate appearance. She imagined herself in it. A captain would look mighty fine being rowed ashore at Nassau in a boat like that.

A commotion started in the aft cabin. She sighed for a moment, looking at the little boat. The sounds increased, and a woman began to scream. Scarlet sighed and headed back, swearing and stamping, bare feet or no.

She undid the latch and threw the cabin door open. The place was a swamp. No one had thought to leave the captives anything as a chamber pot. The two-dozen folk had been using a single wooden soup bowl, and one of the children had tipped it over.

Scarlet shouted for silence. Two women were in tears, one man had a bruised cheek, another bruised knuckles, but they all went quiet, staring at her. Some clutched their children others their spouses, all seemed terrified that something worse was about happen to them. The cabin was very quiet until the little toddling girl saw Scarlet and began to wail, shrieking like the devil himself had come. Scarlet snarled at that, left the open door long enough to snatch a pewter soup-tureen from a pile of plunder, and threw it into the cabin, tossed a couple of threats in after it. When she slammed the door she could still hear the little girl's shrieks.

She fled below.

Pryce and Moreau were systematically dismantling the purser's cabin, throwing broken bits of furniture out into the companionway. The passenger cabins had likewise been stripped, and trails of clothing and personal effects covered the deck. Scarlet found four of her crew with a bottle of brandy in an empty cabin. She confiscated the liquor and set them all back to work, sorting through the mess and packing the more valuable objects up for transport to the *Donny*.

"It would be a sight easer when we go to unload all this if more of us could read or write," she confessed to Pryce ten minutes later as she stood, back in the purser's cabin, dangling the bottle between her fingers.

Pryce licked her lips. "Pass that over here, and I'll write all the labels you want."

"We're under orders and sober."

"One drink *is* sober."

Scarlet passed the bottle, and when Pryce handed it back tipped it and drained it. "You're right, it does a world of good. And just in time. I smell soup, and that has set me right to eat."

Pryce gathered up some paper, ink and a quill, and headed toward the passenger cabins, and Scarlet began hunting through the purser's possessions. She heard Cahill ring the bell for lunch, but kept sorting for just a few more minutes, and then caught a much more ominous sound.

"Sail! Sail ho!" Sunny Jim's voice, from the crow's nest.

She came up on deck and called to him. "What is it?"

"Square topsail, nor'-nor'east, Cap'n."

"Keep your eyes open."

She called down to Burgess, "Sail on the horizon. Get ready to go if we need to."

"Aye, Captain."

She paced, thinking. The visitor was most likely a merchant ship, but merchants didn't look out for each other. The worst a merchant would do, even one that was large and well-armed, would be to flee and report a pirate attack to the authorities. That could take a week or more, and then somebody would have to make up their minds to do something, and beat their way upwind to do it. Not likely to be a problem.

Other pirates were bound by the Code to respect the *Donny's* prize and should, by all rights, keep a respectful distance. But there was always Ned Doyle, who might do anything, and he was not the only fellow who was a violent, lawless fool, only the longest-lived fool. Still, a pirate ship offered few dangers.

But a pirate-hunter, that was another matter. Men like Tavernier, who armed out private warships for the purpose of capturing pirate ships and bringing their very lucrative cargoes home as treasure. An enterprising captain would see a fortune set out before him: the *Donnybrook* with all her crew, each with a price on his or her head, and a captured ship as well. By rights, the *Sparta Queen* was now plunder, and any ship that captured the *Donny* got the *Queen* into the bargain.

That was the danger. Scarlet chewed her lower lip and figured her odds. Nor'-nor-east meant coming in from England, riding down the trades. Not likely a pirate-hunter. Likely a merchant.

Yes, likely a merchant, and they could cut this leaky scow loose and take just her cream, the gold and silver and the silks and fine chinaware and furniture already in the *Donny's* hold, and then take this next ship, rip the gold out of her as well, and head into Nassau port with plenty of coin for the storm season, plenty of money for drink and fun, and never mind two thousand pounds hidden by a skinflint captain who valued money over life itself. Never mind the passengers with all their problems, cattle, husbands, wives, children. And especially never mind a little crying girl who thought Scarlet was a monster.

Scarlet found herself shaking. She wanted to hit something. She wanted a drink even more.

She began to bawl orders.

"Mister Burgess, wrap up your plundering and make ready to move all cargo! Mister Pryce, I want those cabins cleared in twenty minutes, take it or leave it. Mister…" her voice trailed off until she saw the man she was looking for, "Mister Sanchez, get them cows put forward on the *Donny's* crew deck, and move their fodder with them."

"May I bring the milkmaid, too, Cap'n?"

"Only if she hesitates one minute in giving you her cooperation. And Darby, rig the hatch cover for punishment."

That drew a lot of glances from the pirates, but Darby did as he was told, binding the latticed cover for the main hatch upright to a mast, getting ready ropes to hold the victim's wrists while he struggled under the lash. A bucket of seawater set by to throw over the bloodied whip marks.

Finally he stood upright and said, "All set but for the whip, Captain, and I don't know where that is."

Technically, the *Donnybrook* owned a cat-o-nine, but it had been last used well over a year ago, on a man who had refused to take "no" for an answer when dealing with one of his female crewmates.

It had been Flynn's whip, and his job to do the whipping. Scarlet looked around and demanded, "Bring me the *Queen's* bosun."

That officer still stank of bilge water, for he'd been pumping. But he had a steady eye, and Scarlet had no doubt, from the way the *Queen's* sailors looked at him, that she had the right man. A bosun's job was keeping the sails and lines in order, and whipping his fellows when ordered.

"Get the cat out of the bag," Scarlet ordered. "We're about to have a trial, and I think I know how it will end."

The fellow looked her in the eye, measuring, then nodded his head and moved off below, under Darby's supervision. Scarlet called up to Sunny Jim, "How's that sail look?"

"Coming in, Cap'n. Fast, maybe ten knots."

"How far out?"

A long, thoughtful pause. "Two hours, maybe."

"Time enough." Scarlet waited. Darby came back with the bosun, taking a blood-stained whip from its canvas bag.

Scarlet made a trumpet of her hands and began to bellow, "Ship's company to main deck! Ship's company to observe punishment!" Pirates began to shuffle over, curious and wary. Burgess brought the *Queen's* men up from below. Scarlet commanded, "Round up some fellows and get the passengers out here."

That required maneuvering. The passengers ended up on the quarterdeck, hemmed in by pirates with pistols. The *Queen's* sailors were made to sit under guard, and the ship's officers were tied. When the last net of cargo sung over to the *Donny's* deck, Scarlet looked around.

She ought to have a table set up, and sit behind it, official-like. She ought to have her coat. She ought, at least, to be wearing shoes. But it was important to get the thing done while she still could, and that ship, whatever it was, drew closer by the second.

McNamara stood to the forefront of the pirates, his face as stony mask, his eyes burning. Nearby, Bracegirdle was sweating like a pig. Scarlet gave a grim smile at their discomfort, then turned to Mister Yeboah and said, "Go over and bring up Sheffield so we can begin."

The boat was so quiet that the sound of the brig door carried up to the deck. A few moments later Yeboah brought Sheffield over by the scruff of his shirt.

The man tried to keep his dignity around him, but he looked like hell. He's been trapped in the airless brig for a full day, with no food or water, and was already growing gaunt. Sweat drenched his hair and clothes. Like Scarlet, he was barefoot. Scarlet signaled for Yeboah to hold the man still, and began.

"Mister Sheffield…"

"Captain Sheffield." The man's voice was hoarse, but he spoke steady.

Scarlet glared at him. "Mister Sheffield, for I'm captain of your bloody ship now. I may let her go or burn her to the waterline, at my pleasure."

A few of the passengers gasped. Sheffield glowered, but said nothing.

"Mister Sheffield, you are on trial. You stand accused of cutting your men's water ration nearly in half, while continuing to support passengers and cattle. How do you plead?"

Sheffield looked around, as if he didn't quite comprehend what was happening to him. "That's bloody nonsense. It's just running the ship."

Scarlet pitched her voice to carry. "You endangered the lives of your crew in order to avoid discomfort to your passengers. And to… What? Pamper the bloody cows?"

Sheffield raised an angry finger. "The cattle need to be preserved!"

"Them cows was giving nearly three gallons of milk a day, each!" Scarlet moved forward and looked into the man's eyes. "If you'd bothered to cut their water, they'd have suffered no more than to go dry, and your men could have drunk their fill! You cut your men's water so as to have cream for you own tea."

Sheffield's eyes dropped. "I know nothing about cattle. I was told…"

"And no common sense to shore you up? How dare you claim the title 'captain.'?" Scarlet chucked him under the chin with her knuckle, so she could see his eyes as she pronounce sentence. "Twenty lashes, for endangering your crew needlessly, Mister Sheffield, and may God have mercy on your soul."

The sailors shuffled uneasily and voices rose in protest from the passengers, calling for mercy. One of the men said something about "whipping a gentleman," and a woman sobbed, "horrible…"

Scarlet looked fiercely up at them and shouted, "A man's life is worth more than that of a cow."

"My cattle…" began the old woman.

"Your cattle are animals, madam. This men are human, and deserve human dignity and care, though they may have tar on their hands and dirt under their finger nails. They have carried you safe across the ocean, and they deserve your respect."

She got shocked silence for her trouble. Temper rising, she turned back to the grating. Darby had tied Sheffield and ripped the back of his shirt open, but the bosun stood, arms slack, looking confused.

"Well? Scarlet demanded. "Get to it."

The bosun met her eyes. "I will not whip the captain."

Half a dozen thoughts about misplaced loyalty and the chance of reprisals after the *Donnybrook* had sailed away skittered through Scarlett's mind, but she had an easy answer to all of them. Pulling a pistol from her belt, she held it to the bosun's head and told him, "You will beat him like a deck hand, or I will blow out your brains."

The bosun looked at her, swallowed, and went to work, with Darby counting out the strokes. "One. Two. Three..."

On 'six' Sheffield began to groan. At ten he shrieked. The ship was dead silent, except for Sheffield's cries and the sound of the lash. Scarlet felt sweat beginning to run down her cheek. She kept the pistol to the bosun's head.

Most of the men she knew had scars on their backs. She had taken a taken a dozen stripes herself, once.

Blood was running freely down Sheffield's back now. On the fourteenth blow, he went limp against the bindings. Darby stepped forward. "He's fainted."

"Revive him."

Darby flung seawater over the raw wounds, and Sheffield jerked awake. With a glance back at Scarlet, the bosun raised his whip again.

"Cap'n!" It was Sunny Jim.

Scarlet lowered the pistol and turned her gaze aloft. 'What is it?"

"That ship, Cap'n. She's frigate rigged, and coming in fast. There's men in red coats on the deck."

Scarlet's mouth went dry. Royal Marines.

She kept her voice easy. "We have time to finish our work, gentlemen, before we shove off. Mister Darby, I believe the count was fourteen."

Six more blows. The bosun dealt them, Darby counted them, and Sheffield endured them, but Scarlet's mind was out on the horizon with the approaching ship, calculating wind and tide and angles of attack. She barely noticed when Sheffield was cut down.

"Mister Burgess, are we ready to cast off?"

"We have all the cash money and the best of the passengers' things stowed away."

"Mister Pryce, Mister Bracegirdle, Mister McNamara, make ready to cast off. Mister Yeboah, make ready to weigh anchor. Everyone, look to your messmates. We want no one left behind."

A sudden scramble. Pirates leaping to lines and cables, Yeboah calling to the capstan crew, Pryce shouting to stow the cargo crane, passengers screaming, Darby driving the Queen's sailors belowdecks with pistol's drawn.

Cahill came through the crowd with an expression like a thundercloud. "What about my stove?"

Scarlet shook her head. "I am most sorry for it, but it is the stove or our skins. I am most sore in your debt, and will do what I can in future. You must be content with it."

"I was so close."

"That you were. We shall begin better next time. Now get below and put out the fires, for we may have a sea-battle before us."

Above their heads, the cargo crane began to come down, while Yeboah sang out a deep African chant, urging the crew at the capstan to raise the anchor. Scarlet looked around. Where was the Shantyman? If he had become so lazy as to give up singing it would be the last straw.

"A moment, Captain?"

"There you are. Call a capstan shanty and then help get the mainsail up. That frigate's closing fast."

"In only a moment. I need help to move that gig."

Scarlet turned on him in a fury. "Forget the bloody gig! It's a toy, and we don't need it. Now get to work!"

"I shall bring it over by myself, Captain, but if I had help…"

"Why are you so set on that thing?"

The Shantyman looked at her quite seriously and put his hand over his heart. "I feel it in me bones, Captain. We need that thing, and we need it bad."

"I'll help you then." She called a few orders to the pirates hauling on the mainsail, and moved to the gig. If necessary, she would lift it and drop it onto the *Donnybrook*. It must not weigh more than a hundred pounds.

The gig was secured to cleats in the decking, and she slashed the bindings with her belt knife, then crouched and lifted. The Shantyman did the same and the little craft came up easy, revealing an equipment locker under it.

Brand-new locker. New wood, bolted to a middle-aged deck, and locked with a shiny new padlock.

Scarlet wanted to just drop the gig, but the Shantyman held fast, so they carried it to railing and tipped in over the side, into the hands of half a dozen pirates. Scarlet dashed back to the locker.

No time to find the key. She drew the pistol from her belt and pulled the trigger. Nothing but a flash and a puff of smoke. The gun had misfired. She shoved it back into her belt and drew the next.

Sunny Jim called down, "Its' the *Nightingale,* Captain."

What in the name of heaven was the *Nightingale* doing this far northeast?

Scarlet held her next pistol against the padlock and pulled the trigger. Her lead ball tore the lock to pieces, and Scarlet flung open the lid. Inside was a single wooden box. The size of it, and the way it was bound around with iron told her it was a money-chest.

She reached in to lift it out, but it was too heavy for her. Then the Shantyman was reaching too, but even together they could not lift it. Gold was that heavy. Scarlet began to shout for help.

When Yeboah reached over them and pulled the thing clear, the cords on the side of his neck stood out. Somehow the three of them were able to half-lift, half-drag the thing to the *Donnybrook's* deck. Scarlet cut the last line to the *Sparta Queen.* They were free.

Then smoke rose off the *Nightingale's* bow, and a second later water went up in two little splashes, not forty yards away. Cannon balls. Scarlet calculated her angles, watching the ships close. It wasn't over yet.

The *Donnybrook* caught the wind and began to make way, gaining speed. Debris began to be cleared off the deck, chests and barrels and silk dresses, getting stowed below or thrown over the side. Bracegirdle was loading guns. Pryce stood at the wheel. Scarlet shouted to throw up as much canvas as possible, and crews strained at the lines.

In the midst of it all Branna came on deck. "You realize that I still have a pregnant woman in sickbay? Are we holding her for ransom then?"

Scarlet had forgotten about that. She tried to imagine landing in Nassau with a noblewoman and a new baby, and could imagine no good outcome.

The *Nightingale's* guns spoke again, and again there were splashes in the sea, this time much closer. Scarlet could see the crews working the long nines, methodically swabbing and loading. With only a little adjustment the next shots would hit. Her own six-pounders were far outclassed. She measured and felt the wind. The closing angles were inevitable. Her ship would have to endure three shots, maybe four, before they could possibly pull out of range. She could only hope that they didn't lose rigging or take enough hull damage to keep from getting away.

Unless...

Scarlet turned to Branna. "Get her highness out on deck."

"What?"

"Lady what's-her-name. Get her up here on the double. We're putting her out in the captain's gig."

Branna stared about in confusion until her eyes landed on the little green-and-yellow boat, now balanced amidships, atop the *Donny's* own longboat. "That? You're going to put a pregnant woman out in the ocean in that?"

Scarlet caught her by the shoulders and looked at her seriously. "She's in no immediate danger?"

"Not at the moment."

"Then let's put her in it. At the very least she's about to be in a sea battle. And at the very best, Captain

Davenport will be too much of a gentleman to leave a woman in such a situation, and will pause to pick her up."

They got the little gig launched just as the first shots hit home. Two holes in the mainsail would not slow them down. They lowered the boat, its occupant screaming in terror, and shook the last reef from the *Donny's* topsail.

The next round of shot from the nine-pounders was slightly delayed. The then wind changed by four degrees to the north, and Pryce gave the slightest turn to the wheel. The *Donnybrook* ran the length of the *Nightingale's* broadside at extreme range, lost three feet of railing and a little more canvas to her pursuer, and then went into the teeth of the wind, heading for the port at Nassau.

Bracegirdle leaned back against one of his polished brass guns, laughing a little with relief. "Damn, it's been a bloody mad day. I don't think I've ever been so glad not to have to fire a broadside."

Scarlet sat down on the money chest and laughed with him. "All's well as ends, well, I suppose."

"Aye. You know, for a minute there I thought you were going to actually flog McNamara and me, right there on that bloody deck."

Scarlet glared. "Oh, you're still due a flogging, Mister Bracegirdle."

The man stopped and stared, and Scarlet wished, just for a moment, that being captain didn't mean having to keep every single promise she made.

"There will be no flogging without a vote from the crew."

She turned on McNamara. "And how can you be sayin' that?"

"Because that there ship," he pointed toward the *Nightingale* laying over behind them and putting out a boat to bring in the gig, "Ain't chasing us. We are not in chase, or in battle, and we sure ain't sacking that ship, so we're a democracy again. No flogging without a vote of the whole company."

Scarlet considered that. "I believe you are correct, Mister McNamara. But you was still caught fighting on board ship. And I mean to bring it up at the next ship's meeting." She looked up at the sky. "Whenever that is."

The End

But wait, there's more...

The next book in The Pirate Empire

Chapter 1

Storm Season

"Sunny Jim, climb up one more time and tell me again we ain't being followed." Scarlet stood on her ship's broken rail, holding the ratlines in one hand. Her long red hair had come unpinned and whipped behind her in the hot, briny wind.

Burgess, the *Donnybrook*'s quartermaster, shook his head. "Not again. He's told you four times and it must be true, for Sunny Jim has not had a hopeful thought his whole life long. Let it rest, Captain."

Scarlet looked over the faces of her crew, and then back out to the rolling waves behind. "All right. You keep telling me, and it must be so. But that man Davenport's in my dreams. There ain't no reason why he and that damned ship of his should be so far to the nor'east."

"He was too far then. He wouldn't dare come farther," Pryce offered.

Scarlet nodded. "So we say. But that navy bastard is in my dreams, and it means something."

She looked again, but the sea behind them was still empty of all but rolling swells. "All right then. What are we, two days out of Nassau port?" Three?"

Pryce squinted and thought. "Two and a half?" she offered. "Time to get the ship in order."

A few of the pirates groaned, but Scarlet smiled and came off the rail. "Davenport cut us up fierce. We need to make repairs. Every pirate in the Greater Antilles will be hiding in Nassau when the hurricanes blow, and we want to look our best." She called out to the ship's carpenter, who had just come up from below, wiping his damp, bare feet on the dry deck. "Mr. McNamara, how are we set for timber? Can we patch this railing and make her trim?"

McNamara nodded his red-haired head and scratched behind one ear. "We have timber enough for the rail, and canvas to patch the sails. There's even a bit of paint left. We can look right sprightly when we pull into port, if we hop to it."

"Well, then, let's hop!" Pryce grinned and looked at the faces of her crewmates, and then smiled over at Scarlet. "Yes?"

"So we shall! Let's clean her up and go in like the pirates we are, with sails set and the black flag flying. Aye?" She looked to the crew, and began to see signs of agreement. "Aye?" Men and women together nodded and smiled. "Well then?" asked Scarlet. "Shall we fix the old *Donnybrook* up and make her fine?"

A cheer rose, and the pirates began to laugh and slap each other on the back, remembering boisterous times in years gone by. Scarlet shouted, "To Nassau Port!" and stood basking in the cheers. But as she did, her eyes strayed back to the horizon, watching.

...to be continued

Be sure to enjoy
The next installment in The Pirate Empire

Storm Season

Book reviews are the best way to let an author know how you feel about their work. Please consider providing an Amazon review, for the benefit of both the author and future readers.

Made in the USA
San Bernardino, CA
29 December 2018